Miriam Dunne lives on Sherkin Island in County
Cork with her husband and three children. This is
her first novel.

'Reads like a breath of the freshest air . . . hilarious,
poignant and truly compassionate' *IT Magazine*

'Miriam Dunne has a good eye' *The Times Literary
Supplement*

'A first novel to be proud of – funny, moving and
truthful' *Ireland on Sunday*

Blessed Art Thou
A Monk Swimming

Miriam Dunne

review

Copyright © 1997 Miriam Dunne

The right of Miriam Dunne to be identified as the Author of
the Work has been asserted by her in accordance with the
Copyright, Designs and Patents Act 1988.

First published in 1997
by REVIEW
An imprint of Headline Book Publishing

First published in paperback in 1998

10 9 8 7 6 5 4 3 2 1

ISBN 0 7472 5847 3

Typeset by Palimpsest Book Production Limited,
Polmont, Stirlingshire
Printed and bound in Great Britain by
Clays Ltd, St Ives plc

Headline Book Publishing
A division of Hodder Headline PLC
338 Euston Road
London NW1 3BH

For Syd

Chapter 1

Another ball came over the asylum wall and bounced around before coming to rest by the side of the road. It was the ninth that day. I picked it up to add to my collection. It was hard and black with an elephant stamped on it. There were always more about after an escape, as if liberating the balls was the only chance of freedom for those left behind.

The whole neighbourhood was talking about last night's escape. Mr Moran from Number Ten knew all about it. He worked nights at the asylum dismantling wardrobes assembled the day before by the occupational therapy unit. The numbered parts had to be packed into boxes complete with instructions and left ready to be reassembled on the next day.

The job was risky with all the tools lying about and Mr Moran often got attacked by the odd loony creeping up behind him. The one who'd escaped this time thought he was Admiral Lord Nelson. He refused to assemble wardrobes and used the wood instead to build himself a boat. He worked so hard Mr Moran hadn't the heart to interfere. He got caught up in it himself and scoured Dublin in his lunch hour for the necessary parts. The boat got so big it had to be carried out to the exercise yard. When it was almost built, Mr Moran, a civil servant by day, took the afternoon off to see to the rigging. When it was finished the Governor and staff came out for a look. Mr Moran was praised for encouraging Nelson to abandon wardrobes and use his obvious talents as a boat builder. Everyone was astonished next day to see the boat fully rigged and Admiral Lord Nelson gone for good. He'd nipped up the mast and over the wall during the night and escaped down our road.

Bird Avenue where we lived was once part of a large estate. The old house still stood, but the grounds were taken up by two rows of semis, the asylum and its twenty-foot wall. I'd been sitting under it all morning. Now the balls had stopped coming and a wind was getting up. I watched the clouds race before the sun and cast shadows that billowed up the road like waves. Everyone else was at school. The only sign of life was the breadman in his horse and cart pulling away from the Lukes' house where he stopped every day for his dinner. I didn't want to go home till he called at our house as I knew my mother would be going mad waiting for the cakes she ordered every Friday which was a Fast day and meant you couldn't eat meat.

'What in the name of God does he be doing stuck in Lukes' till three?' she'd fume. 'Of course it's a different story when Mr Luke's off sick, then everyone gets their bread on time.'

'Maybe Mrs Luke's too busy to cook him dinner when her husband's ill,' I'd try to reason.

'Dinner my foot,' was all she'd say.

Our house was quiet when I got in except for the coals shifting in the fire. My mother sat dozing, her face relaxed into the folds of her neck. I helped myself to the remains of Friday's dinner, tinned salmon salad, cocktail onions and beetroot. There was nothing left in the cake box. The knife slid off my plate and clattered into the grate when I sat on the pouffe.

My mother woke with a start. 'Oh, it's only you,' she yawned, her top set of teeth falling down as she did so.

'What happened to the cakes?' I asked, knowing she'd got carried away and eaten the lot.

Her yawn vanished. 'What dropped?' she asked ignoring my question.

I held up the knife.

'That's a man to the house. Thank God it's not a spoon. I wonder who it'll be?'

A dropped spoon meant a disappointment. A knife or a fork meant a visit from a man or a woman. I noticed her legs had gone all mottled from the heat of the fire and thought it a pity as they were a nice shape.

'What do I care at my age,' she said when I told her and tugged her skirt down. 'And would you ever leave me alone, haven't I enough to contend with, what with your Daddy slipping out without leaving a penny for Celine's shoes and that lunatic escaping, and now the nuns not wanting you back.' She sighed. 'Things always come in threes and that's an end of it, I hope. Touch wood,' she added and gripped the arms of the chair.

We heard the gate. My mother with fear in her eyes shot up in spite of her bulk and went to look. 'It's Rowan or Owen from next door,' she said with relief, peering from behind the curtain.

'Which one?'

'I don't know. They both look the same.'

It was true. Rowan and Owen looked identical. They were Irish twins, born in the same year.

'There'll be no stopping them now since they bought the big house,' my mother went on. 'And to think it could have been ours if your Daddy'd only more go in him. Gertie Freeney'll never do it justice. For all her money she's that common. Always round here borrowing cups of sugar. A whole packet I wouldn't mind but cups.'

'Rowan's hair's curlier,' I told her.

My mother opened the window and went to the piano. 'Think I'll play a few tunes before I tackle the washing up.'

My mother loved showing off on the piano. It was her only weapon against the Freeneys next door. Gertie Freeney was rolling in it but she hadn't a note. When my mother played, Gertie shut her windows, mad with envy. She'd retaliated by putting her daughter on the piano in the hope that one day she'd catch up.

'Have you seen the yellow waltz album?' my mother asked, rooting in the piano stool.

'There's no point,' I said. 'They're out next door and Rowan and Owen haven't a clue about music.'

'Can I not play for my own enjoyment?' she said, and went off in a huff to answer the back door.

'If it's Rowan I'm not in,' I called after her and stopped to listen on the stairs. Rowan was all right, but too intense. Sometimes he shook when you got too close to him. Once he accused me of preferring his brother because I smiled at Owen before putting my bathing cap on.

'Hello, is it Rowan? No? Come in, Owen,' she called out. 'Marian, you're wanted down here.

'She's left Muckross School,' I heard her say. 'I had to take her away, it's gone downhill so much since they built Corporation houses next door. Not that any of them could afford that kind of money.'

Liar, I thought; she'd spent a whole morning trying

to persuade the nuns to take me back. They told her I was a bad apple who might contaminate the rest.

Owen leant against the sink hugging his elbows. A lock of fair hair covered one eye. 'Are you coming out?' he asked and flicked it back.

'No, I've just got in, but come up and see my pageant costume if you want.'

'OK.' He shrugged, not sounding keen.

Owen liked kissing best. It lasted for hours, he hated if you moved, it ruined his concentration. It wasn't so bad if there was something going on behind him to look at, but usually there wasn't.

My mother started on the piano as we went upstairs. At least it was better than the sound of washing up with cutlery being fired into the drawer. She'd developed a skill at aiming each knife, fork and spoon into the right compartment. It relieved her of the daily tedium she said.

I asked Owen to wait on the landing and went into the bathroom to change. Stripping down to my knickers, I took my bird costume out of the hot press. It was covered in black silky feathers and swept down to the floor. Before putting it on I called to Owen.

He stopped still in the doorway and stared, then, coming over, ran his finger gently over my appendix scar. The look on his face was interesting. Our eyes held and there wasn't a sound except for his breathing. Then we noticed the piano'd stopped.

'Don't move,' Owen whispered and left the room. He called to my mother. 'That was great, Mrs O'Dea. Can you play some more?'

'Did you like it, Owen?'

I heard him reassuring her and slipped into my costume as the music started again.

5

'What have you done?' Owen stood in the doorway looking flushed.

'Don't you like it?' I twirled round.

'Not as much as the other.' His voice sounded gruff. He cleared his throat.

'Wait till you see my wings.' I slipped past him into the bedroom and got a box from under the bed. Owen followed and before I could get them on he pulled me down on the bed. We started to kiss. Something hard pressed against me. I knew there wasn't anything in his pocket and thought of male ballet dancers leaping about in their skin tights, glancing off the ballerinas but never touching. Between the feathers and silk eiderdown we sank slowly to the floor bringing the box down with us. The piano stopped again; we held our breaths as my mother called.

'What are you two up to?'

'Christ,' Owen said and went out the door. 'Don't stop now, Mrs O'Dea, that was smashing,' I heard him tell her.

'Oh go on, Owen, you're only saying it.'

'No really, Mrs O'Dea, I liked it. I bet you couldn't play the whole thing straight through without stopping?'

'Indeed I could, Owen, but you'd soon be bored.'

'I wouldn't, Mrs O'Dea, honest, I'd love it.'

'Well, if you're sure then I'll play one of my new pieces. Which would you like? There's "Tales from the Vienna Woods" or "Kitten on the Keys"?'

'Could you not play them both?'

I didn't hear any more as I locked myself in the bathroom and started to undress.

The doorknob rattled and Owen called. 'Open up, Marian, let's in.'

I asked him to quit shouting or my mother would hear, but he kept on.

'C'mon, be a sport, open the door.'

'Not now, Owen, I can't, you'd better go down and listen to the music.' I laughed and turned the bath on full. The geyser flared up and pumped hot water into the bath. My mother hated the word geyser and told us to call it the Ascot. My sister and I were not encouraged to take baths. Our father believed they weakened the constitution and our mother thought we'd be overcome by steam and drown. She'd never learnt to swim and once, when stepping on to a boat, fell into the sea in her Sunday best. The man she was with didn't move a muscle to help. Another of her reasons not to trust men.

Men, she claimed, were only after the one thing. She'd said it so many times I didn't listen any more. I wasn't even sure what she meant. The only thing I could think of was something awful like the man wanting to pee into the woman's tummy button.

I lay back in the water and watched my newly sprouted breasts break the surface. They still felt strange. Six months ago I had nothing and wrote in desperation to a bust-developing agency in England who guaranteed a forty-inch chest or your money back. I didn't want anything that size. A girl's in school were so huge they knocked against you when you walked next to her. She didn't play hockey because they bounced so much when she ran and a whack from a ball meant instant cancer. She always got asked up at tennis club hops, though.

The doorknob turned. It was my mother. 'Are you there, Marian? Don't tell me you're taking a bath? What did you lock the door for? It's dangerous.'

I ignored her. She was always terrified something

drastic would happen to us, especially my sister. But then her first child died soon after he was born. He was never baptised and went straight to Limbo. Limbo's a place where you have to stay for ever. You never get to see God so it's no use praying for anyone there. Not like the souls in Purgatory. When they need prayers to get them closer to Heaven their agonising cries are muffled by the vast distance between us. By the time their cries reach us, all you can hear is a high-pitched ringing in your ear. It only takes one Hail Mary for the ringing to stop. My parents would never talk about our dead brother. It probably upset them. But it disturbed me to think he hadn't a name. They wouldn't say where he was buried and couldn't even remember his birthday.

My mother banged on the door. 'Are you there, Marian?'

I said I was and asked if Owen had left.

'He has, and d'you know you were wrong about him. He's really keen on music, he loved my playing. He's coming back again tomorrow. I think I'll go down and practise a bit more.'

I waited till she'd gone for my favourite part of the bath when I pull out the plug and lie back watching the water recede with great gurglings as it sucks down the hole. There's a pause and a loud wail as it draws breath for the next surge. It goes on, over and over again and I listen, mesmerised, till the last drop has gone, leaving me naked on the white enamel.

Chapter 2

I woke up to the sound of the front door banging and my mother crying out in the bed beside me. She bounded over to the window and called out.

'Larry, Larry, the money you promised . . .'

Her voice faded as she backed away from the curtains, dismayed at revealing herself to the neighbourhood.

'He couldn't have got down the road that quick,' she muttered.

We heard whistling on the stairs.

'Did you call, Kitty?' My father came in freshly shaved and smelling of Old Spice. The room suddenly felt brighter.

'My God, Larry, you did it on purpose.'

'What?' he asked innocently.

'You knew I needed money for today and you pretended to leave the house and I'm after making a fool of myself calling out the window after you.'

She stood there fuming, a row of metal curlers clamped to her head like mantraps and secured by a brown hairnet which came over her forehead. Her cheeks were hollow without her teeth and a kimono covered in red dragons hung from her shoulders.

'I was only letting the cat out. Now get back into bed and I'll bring you some tea.'

He winked at me and went out. We didn't have a cat, my mother couldn't abide animals in the house. He was always saying daft things like that.

My mother got back into bed. It was one from my father's shop. He sold lots with an ad he had of an old lady stuffing money in a mattress and a slogan which said: 'Put your money in an O'Dearest.'

My mother sighed. 'That Gertie Freeney, has she nothing better to do than stand at the gate all day gossiping. I bet she's showing off the new car. Did you know they got another? The old one wasn't good enough, and yet when they came here first they had to stick paper on their windows, they couldn't afford curtains. He was only an unestablished civil servant and now look at them.'

Gertie Freeney had everything. A husband, Basil, who donned an apron after work and waited on her hand and foot, a new rig-out for every season, and a car that swept her off to Mass every Sunday when my mother had to bicycle uphill in all weathers. Once, late at night when my mother was out hanging clothes on the line, she spotted Basil in the back of the car with his eyes closed and his face pressed white against the window. She thought he was dead and raised the alarm. Gertie never forgave her for spreading it round that she worked him to death and he hid in the car to get away from her.

'Have you seen Gertie's upper arms lately?' my mother asked, sounding almost cheerful. 'They're turning into large hams from lack of use. No rig-out in the world could disguise them, especially in summer.'

'Here, Kitty, drink it while it's hot.' My father came in with the tea and told me breakfast was ready.

'Is Celine up?' I asked.

'No, the coast's clear, we're the only early birds.' He smiled.

My father had hung pictures of Lourdes on the wall all the way down the stairs. There was one of Our Lady in the grotto surrounded by crutches, proof of the miracles she granted daily. My father was devoted to her and had made the pilgrimage five times.

The table was set for two by the window. Outside a trim lawn ran down to a wall where my beech tree grew. 'Here we are, done to a turn.' My father carried in plates of rashers on his special fried bread. He'd been warned off all fats by the doctor and fried his bread in milk instead of dripping.

'What's your plan for today?' he asked and began to eat as if he'd been starved.

'I've got to find a new school.'

'Can't it wait? Why not come into the shop for the day and I'll take you out to lunch. We could go to the North Star.'

'I can't,' I said, annoyed that he wouldn't take school seriously. Everyone else's parents did. Mine never even looked at my reports. They were terrible. Apart from English and Art I never got more than ten out of a hundred for anything. Then I started adding noughts, giving myself full marks or honours but they didn't even notice till I pointed it out to them.

'Go on then, find yourself a school if that's what you want, but don't pick a fancy one with too many uniforms.' He put his hand over mine and squeezed it gently. 'Eat up now and would you look at the birds. I put some bread out and they're hopping mad for it.'

He watched with pleasure, his face fine and thin, the temples visible from his receding hair. A blue vein stood out on his forehead reminding me of death. I asked him about it and his hand went straight to it.

'What d'you mean, where?'

'It doesn't mean you're getting old, does it?' I kept on, knowing it would upset him but needing reassurance.

'What gave you that idea?' He sounded agitated and, wiping his mouth, got up quickly. 'Have to go, it's late.' We hugged at the door but I'd spoilt the breakfast.

My father was terrified of death and had locked himself in a room for a week when his mother died. When anyone he knew died he went on a binge that lasted for days.

A noise came from upstairs. Someone was getting up, so I went out to the beech tree. My beech tree was huge. Its branches stretched over walls and hedges into other people's gardens. With the help of a rope I pulled myself up the massive trunk and settled into the centre where no one could see me.

Finding a school would have to wait till my sister Celine went out. She was going to be an actress and was very highly strung. My mother said this was due to her artistic temperament and excused her of everything. Proof of her artistic temperament stood mounted on a mahogany shield on top of the piano. There were bronze medals at first, then silver followed by the gold. Now she was going in for the Record Cup, the highest award of the Father Mathew Feis.

A fortune teller told my mother that one day she'd sit back and applaud one of her daughters. 'Which one?' I asked, but all she said was, 'You mark my words, Marian, Celine will be a star one day and all this will have been worth it.'

I heard a scream from the house that meant he'd gone off without leaving any money.

They were in the kitchen. My mother stood stock-still by the sink, a plate of toast in smithereens at her feet. Behind on the wall an egg slithered to the floor. Celine was red in the face and yelling at my mother.

'You fool, you know I can't wear pink satin for Deirdre of the Sorrows. I must have black.' Then Celine caught hold of the door and banged it three times. My mother winced and begged her to stop and think of the neighbours.

'Feck the neighbours,' Celine yelled and darted upstairs. With relief we heard her door slam.

My mother dried her hands and got out her purse. 'It's all your daddy's fault, he never left the money. Now you'll have to go next door and ring him from Gertie's. Tell him he's to call into Bradley's at lunchtime and get a pair of black leather ballet shoes size five. Tell him he needn't come home without them. And here, while you're at it, slip into the church and give this to St Joseph. He's never yet failed me.' She pressed a ten-shilling note into my hand. 'It's for Celine's success,' she added, seeing my puzzled look.

Before I could protest we heard a crash from upstairs. I followed my mother up without a word. The minute she opened her door Celine started to yell, 'Get out, get out, leave me alone.'

She sat hunched on the bed, her white portable radio smashed to pieces on the floor. I felt sorry for it, it'd been so pretty once. My mother went to close the windows.

'Please keep your voice down, Gertie's in the garden.'

'What do I care, let her hear, let them all hear.' Celine leapt off the bed, and, pushing her aside, opened the windows again. They wrestled together and got caught up in the net curtains. Celine screamed as if she were being murdered every time she got them open. Some kids gathered outside to watch. I sneaked downstairs hoping Owen wouldn't come and went out the back.

Gertie was on the phone. I could tell from the posh voice she had on through the half-open door. You could never be sure of Gertie because of the drink. She never got really drunk sipping sherry all day, but it mounted up as I discovered once when playing hide and seek with Owen. I'd opened a wardrobe and an avalanche of bottles fell out. Owen found me at once with all the noise.

She came into the kitchen. 'Oh, it's you,' she said, squinting from the cigarette in her mouth. 'Work away,' she said when I asked could I use the phone. She began slicing chips. Before I could get out the door she started moaning about Rowan's appetite.

'He won't eat a thing, only muck so I bought this chipper that puts frills on in the hope that he'll eat them.' She held one up to demonstrate.

'That's nice,' I said edging past her. I couldn't imagine Rowan being so fussy. He was so boring. The only interesting thing about him was the way he peed on Gertie's roses. She couldn't understand why they turned yellow and died.

My father sounded vague on the phone. He said he'd see about the shoes, so I told him there'd been a scene, the whole neighbourhood had heard, and life would be hell if he didn't get them. He was silent for a bit and then asked if I'd go for a walk up the mountains on Sunday as it was his only day off. I said I'd see, but what about the shoes. He said he'd try, but had to go as a customer had come in. After that I rang a few schools pretending to be my mother and asked if they'd send on a prospectus.

* * *

My footsteps echoed through the empty church. The only sign of life came from the Perpetual Light glowing in front of the altar like a watchful eye. I gave the money to St Joseph and sat for a while lapping up the peace and quiet. Our Lord in red robes and Our Lady in blue stood in alcoves either side of the altar. Saints on pedestals looked down imploringly or raised their eyes to heaven.

There was a saint for everything. Saint Anthony for finding things, Saint Blaise for throats, Saint Christopher for journeys and Saint Jude for hopeless cases. My patron saint was Saint Catherine of Siena. I'd taken her for Confirmation so my third name was Catherine. The Catherine wheel was called after her. Imagine being tied to a wheel, set on fire and rolled down a rocky hill. It was worse though for my father's patron saint, Saint Polycarp of Smyrna. He had his arms and legs tied to four different horses. They were sent galloping in all directions. Then his bits were burned in four separate fires. It'd be difficult for him to rise up on the last day, I thought. But it'd be just as difficult if you were a skeleton, or a half-rotten corpse, or even a handful of dust. It'd be better if you'd just died. Thinking about it was a nightmare. Everyone who'd been born, rising from the ground, hobbling on sticks or bits of old bone, lining up waiting to be judged. And the wails of those condemned to everlasting flames. Not my idea of a joyful reunion with loved ones. Suppose you went to heaven and your parents ended up in hell? How could you be happy? I'd asked about it in Christian Doctrine class and was told I'd feel different when the time came.

When I got home I found my mother in the shed still in her dressing gown.

'We're locked out,' she said handing me the rake and avoiding my eyes.

'How come?' I asked.

'Celine didn't want me in the house while she was getting ready, I was getting on her nerves. Then she went out the front and must have forgotten. I couldn't go after her,' she added as if this explained everything.

'She's insane,' I began but my mother turned on me.

'Never use that word in this house. D'you hear? That's a terrible thing to say about your own sister.'

She was so angry it reminded me of the time the doctor told her Celine was unbalanced. He'd got it wrong of course. Like all men, he didn't understand. It was just Celine's artistic temperament coming out. She made me swear never to tell anyone, especially my father.

I climbed up on the window and, easing the rake through the top, lowered it carefully. The catch clicked open as usual.

Chapter 3

The safest place after the beech tree was bed where I could lose myself in a book or just lie and dream. When my father came home, my favourite dream was that our house would rise into the sky and fly away to a place where Celine couldn't find us. All she'd find when she got home was an empty space where the house had once been.

Once I dreamt that a giant bed stretched the length of our road, all the way up to the asylum wall and everyone from Bird Avenue slept in it together. Everybody's parents had separate beds except the Hansons who lived opposite. They were the only happy family I knew. I practically lived in their house. The parents were so young and easy-going. They never made a fuss about anything. One of their children, a big boy of ten, spent mealtimes sitting on his father's shoulders for weeks eating from a plate balanced on his father's head. He came down eventually, and no one ever said a word.

'Since you're so enamoured with them, why don't you pack your bags and move over there altogether and be done with it,' my mother said sarcastically. We used to play for hours in the tall trees at the end of their garden. They belonged to the adjoining estate. We hung swings and bars, old tyres and ropes from the overhanging branches and gave acrobatic displays pretending we were a circus.

Once some children staying at the big house came to watch. After a bit one of them called out, 'You must be very poor, none of you wears vests underneath except for her,' and she pointed to me. We all stopped and jumped down as they'd spoilt our fun. As we left, Kath, the eldest, shouted to them, 'I'm not poor, my family is related to the Queen.' She didn't need to say that, I thought, and never felt the same about her again.

Eventually the Hansons moved out when their house got too small. Years later my mother met Mrs Hanson at a baby show. She looked a wreck and appealed to my mother. 'What am I going to do, Mrs O'Dea? I've ten now and I'm only thirty-four.'

We only had three bedrooms in our house so I had to share with my mother. We hardly met, though, as she stayed up till all hours doing housework. In the mornings I got up if she lay on, and she got up if I lay on. One morning she came in with the post and snapped, 'Stop picking your nose behind that book.'

'What's keeping it up then?' I asked, showing her my two hands holding it. But she ignored this and went off without a word. I opened the envelopes she'd tossed on the bed. Only two schools had replied, one in Stephen's Green, and the other an amazing-looking castle by the sea. They were both Loreto convents.

My mother was rooting under the stairs when I went to show her. 'Not now, I haven't my glasses.' She sat back on her haunches and sighed. 'Where could those damn papers have got to? I must look up Celine's horoscope.'

'Will I ring them and make an appointment?' I asked. She ignored me. 'Just run upstairs, Marian, and see if there's any newspapers in the hotpress.' She rose stiffly to her feet and carried the ironing board into the dining room.

'I can't,' I said following her. 'Celine's in the bathroom, she won't let me near it. What's wrong with her anyway, didn't she get her ballet shoes?'

'She did. It's her eyebrows, she can't get them on. She should never have shaved them off in the first place, but don't let on I said anything.'

We heard footsteps on the stairs. My mother held up a warning finger then spat on it, and struck the iron to test for heat. It hissed as Celine came in with her vanity case and sat by the window. I ignored her and asked my mother what was the best time to make an appointment.

'Appointment for what?' she asked with a frown.

'With the schools I was telling you about. There's Loreto on the Green and . . .'

'The Green? That's out, it's too dark. Your daddy sent Celine there once but he took her away again when he discovered the sun never shone that side of the Green.'

'Well, the other then, it's farther away, but they take boarders.'

'Why should she be allowed to go to boarding school when I was never sent?' Celine asked, filing her nails with a pout.

'But you never wanted to go, dear, and you did so well where you were, passed all your exams, the nuns were full of praise. Anyway Marian's only romancing, your father'd never sanction it what with all the expense.'

'It's not only that,' I said. 'He wouldn't let me go anyway.'

My mother smiled as she draped Celine's dress over a chair and stood back to admire it.

The thought of going away to school excited me. Boarding schools in Enid Blyton were like one big happy family. Even getting into trouble for being out of bounds or having midnight feasts sounded fun, and the mean girls always got sorted out in the end.

Startled, I looked up to find Celine standing over me.

'You blind bat, you never noticed my new top,' she said angrily.

I had noticed it and thought the orange colour vile. It made her skin look ghastly.

'Bitch,' she said as if reading my thoughts and dug her nails into my arm. I pushed her off, but she left the room quickly, banging the door behind her. When I went to follow, my mother barred the way.

'Leave it, she's upset, it's the strain of the Feis.'

'What about me?' My voice rose, but she looked weary and asked me to get her a glass of water as she was parched from ironing.

'Let it run till it gets really cold,' she called after me in the kitchen. I turned the tap on full and waited.

Bertha, my old doll, sat eyeless in the window, the sole survivor after Celine attacked the whole family of them with a spade. I'd found them all with faces smashed and eyes dangling inside their heads. Except for her eyes Bertha had escaped, but was still waiting to be sent off to the Dolls' Hospital for new ones.

It was Celine's revenge after I'd pounced on her with my mother's fox stole over my head. The fox was real, with bushy tail, claw feet, glass eyes and snout. Celine went mad with rage. I had to lock myself in the bedroom to escape. She took it out on my dolls but I knew it was me she really wanted to kill. I never played a trick on her again and always made sure not to be in the house with her alone. It was all right when she was asleep, but the minute I heard the bedsprings creak I was straight out the door.

Celine stayed in for the rest of the day so I went to bed with a book to be out of the way. A cloud hung over the house whenever she was at home. Luckily she wasn't in much between acting and the boyfriend. She was doing a heavy line with a dentist, Richard Bouchier-Hawes. She called him Chard. They spent most of their time beagling. That was just like hunting but without any horses. Maybe he can't afford any, I said to my mother. Nonsense, she said. He'd a double-barrelled name and his family had been mentioned in Social and Personal. Besides, Chard wouldn't risk letting Celine on a horse, he was that mad about her. Maybe he would later, I thought, if he was fool enough to marry her. I felt sorry for him really, but he ought to have seen through her by now. The cracks were beginning to show. Especially at night when he drove her home. Sometimes she'd flounce out, slam the door, tear off the silver bracelet he'd given her and fling it back at him. My mother always went out later with a torch to retrieve it, but it'd been thrown back so many times now it was all puckered with dents.

I must have fallen asleep as I heard myself moan before I woke with the nightmare feeling.

'What's up?' my mother asked.

She was sitting up in bed reading with a plate of crackers on her chest. Usually I hated waking when she was there, as she never wore her teeth in bed, and the steady munch of her gums nearly drove me insane.

When I told her about the nightmare she patted the eiderdown without losing her place.

I sat up. Everything looked normal. The room we

shared was packed with furniture from the shop. A dressing table, tallboy, wardrobe and two beds; there was barely room to walk.

I lay down again and everything went small, the way it does through the wrong end of the binoculars. I was afraid to go to sleep in case the nightmare came back. It was always the same. My body turned completely inside out and I had to go around with all the raw ends, tubes and jangly bits exposed to the world. I could never get back again and sometimes woke up screaming. 'Are you turning off the light?' I asked, alarmed to see my mother folding her newspaper.

'In a minute,' she said taking out her hairnet.

'Would you not leave it on?' I asked, but she refused saying we'd never get any sleep. 'Can I come in with you then?' I asked, knowing it'd be pitch dark as the street lights had gone off long ago. She agreed as long as I lay still. I squeezed in beside her, snuggling into her back. Without a corset she felt soft and fat. Except for her breathing there wasn't a sound. I matched my breath with hers but couldn't keep up. She was still on the way up when I was coming down. Trying to keep in time left me breathless. Then she stopped breathing.

I lifted my head off the pillow and stared into the darkness, straining to hear in the silence. I nudged her urgently, and asked her to breathe but she wouldn't. I knew it was only an act, she'd done it before, but each time I dreaded it might be real. I was afraid she might suffocate from holding her breath, or that her brain cells would die from lack of oxygen. Maybe that's why she's so thick, I thought, and prodded her angrily with my elbow, but she wouldn't budge. I jerked the covers away to let in the cold air and put my face against hers, but there wasn't a trace of breathing.

'I know you're not dead, please breathe for me, please,' I begged, hating myself for it. The blood throbbed in my ears and lights flashed behind my eyes as I tried to focus on something.

'Didn't even a little bit of you think I was dead?' Her voice startled me.

'I knew you were pretending, I wish you wouldn't, I hate it.'

'Will you miss me when I'm gone?' she went on.

'Of course I will.'

'How much will you miss me, a big bit or a little bit?' she kept on like a child needing reassurance.

'Don't talk about it please, I can't bear it,' I begged and went back to my own bed.

She was snoring in no time but I couldn't sleep. I wondered what made her like that? She was so miserable and bad-tempered most of the time. And she cried a lot, a low mournful sound like an animal. I felt sorry for her at first to find her huddled in a dark room, but it annoyed me in the end as she wouldn't say what was wrong. She never did it when the others were around.

When I thought about it I realised that all the women in Bird Avenue were a bit queer. Most of them stayed at home and didn't go out to work. Whenever my mother talked about the time she worked in England she went in raptures. She was a flower arranger and window dresser in a department store in Surrey. To hear her go on about it you'd think it was the greatest thing that ever happened to her.

'What made you come back if it was all so wonderful?' I asked irritated by the wistful look on her face. It was as if returning to Ireland, marrying my father and having us was the biggest mistake of her life.

'I had to. My mother made me. She needed someone

to look after her in her old age,' she said, sounding like a little girl.

That wasn't true. There was a maiden aunt who looked after my grandmother.

'You were a grown woman, what did you listen to her for?'

'In my day, Marian, everyone did what their mother said.'

More fool they, I thought, infuriated by the resigned look on her face.

I lay awake for a while and made a tour of Bird Avenue in my mind.

Number One – Mrs Carroll. Secret drinker. Husband and older son have upped and left. Youngest son in the asylum.

Number Four – Terrified of having more babies. Only smiles when husband is away. Lucky for her he's a commercial traveller.

Number Seven – Us.

Number Eight – Gertie.

Number Ten – Puts all her hopes in her two daughters. Both entered for every competition going – dancing, drama, singing and piano. House full of trophies, cups and medals. Beats them with orange box sticks if they don't practise. Their legs destroyed with splinters. Gives them special medicine for rosy cheeks and curls their blonde hair into fat ringlets. Both made to smile all the time so the judges find them irresistible. Youngest was at the bus stop one day going to a Fancy Dress as a doll in a box. Box too wide so bus queue and conductor had to force her through.

Number Thirteen – Attempted suicide. Found by milkman with her head in the oven.

Number Sixteen – Chalk-white face. Afraid to go

outside. Her husband, the Guard, tries to persuade her to walk as far as the gate. If there's a dog in sight she flees back inside.

Number Nineteen – Ex-teacher. Keeps her children studying day and night. Says it's an investment for their future. Can't bear stupid people. She asked me once to look up the number of the local pharmacy. Flew into a rage when I started looking under 'F'. 'Very little between the ears,' I heard her muttering as she snatched the book away.

I stayed awake a little longer, wondering why I was so thick but must have drifted off as I never got beyond number nineteen.

Chapter 4

My father was adamant at first. Boarding school was out, did I think he was made of money? But I kept on. Suppose I had a vocation? The only way to test it was by spending time in a convent. After all, if Our Lady was calling me how could I refuse her? In the end he gave in.

My mother made the appointment with the nuns and I was to start school the following week. She came home grumbling about the clothes list.

'Four pairs of leather shoes and three sets of everything else, with name tags sewn on the lot. I ask you, Marian, how in the name of God am I going to get cutlery and napkin rings stamped with your initials, they must mean silver?'

My father said the nuns certainly had fancy ideas, especially when they didn't have to fork out for it themselves.

To save on expense we borrowed a trunk from a neighbour, Mrs Carroll, at Number One. Her son's initials, W.C., were painted in large white letters on both sides. Willie wouldn't be needing it any more now that he was locked up in the asylum. Willie had tried to murder his mother twice. After the initial shock, Mrs Carroll consoled herself there was only a twenty-foot-high wall between them and she could visit whenever she liked. He wouldn't leave her like the others. Nobody could remember her husband he'd been away so long in America. Her eldest had emigrated to Australia. Some said it was the farthest place he could find to get away from her.

My last day was a Sunday, the worst day in our house when everyone was at home together. As usual, I got up early to get my father's breakfast. He thought it a great treat having it in bed, but I only did it to keep him away from the others.

I sounded the gong in the hall. Two short taps and one long. Our special signal to give him time to go to the bathroom and put his teeth in. The smell of Hafner's sausages wafted up the stairs. My father brought them home every Saturday for a treat. They had browned nicely under the grill and I slid them on to the plate. The plate, an antique from the shop, had a hollow base with a little funnel that you filled with hot water to keep the food warm. I wet the tea and added a jug of hot water to the tray so he'd have no excuse for coming down.

He was sitting up in bed waiting for me, his hands resting on the turned-down sheet. When I set the tray down in front of him he gave me a strange look.

'What's up?' I asked.

'Nothing, Mar. It's just that you're growing up so well. That scarf suits your fair hair.' He frowned. 'Only don't tell Celine I said so, will you?'

I glanced in the mirror, annoyed to think he was afraid to pay me a compliment for fear of offending Celine. Yes, the blue silk wasn't bad. It was a present from an Italian student staying at Gertie's. He was amazed at finding Irish girls unchaperoned and bought the scarf in gratitude. All he ever did was kiss me and whisper Bella, bella, bella in my ear.

I drew the curtains and opened the window.

'Looks a grand day,' my father said buttering his toast. 'Care for a walk on your last Sunday?'

'I dunno, there's some name tags to be sewn on.'

I stared out the window remembering when we'd always spent Sundays together. It was his only day off. First thing in the morning, I'd be into his bed and we'd snuggle up while he made up these stories about a giant who lived up the mountains. The giant only came down at night when everyone was asleep to play tricks on the people in the Avenue. He lifted the roofs off the houses and took everyone from their beds, switching them around, so all the families were mixed up. When they woke up next morning there was total confusion.

We heard a thump on the wall and my mother calling out.

'What does she want now?' he asked.

'Money for the papers,' I told him.

'Help yourself.' He nodded to his coat in the wardrobe.

I always got money for my mother whenever I could. Otherwise there'd be a row. Whatever he gave her, was never enough.

I took some change from his pocket and went into her room. She was getting ready for Mass and turned to me in a panic.

'I'll never make half ten. What time is it, Marian? No, don't tell me.' She jerked her head around trying to get her earrings on. 'Is your father up yet?'

'He's having breakfast.'

'Blast these bloody fiddly things. I can't find the hole.'

I clicked two half-crowns down on the dressing table. She looked at them in disgust.

'If that's all you can get for me, I'll have to go in myself.'

'No don't. I'll get more,' I promised but I knew it was plenty. The Sunday papers only came to two and six.

She muttered something about rightful dues as I left.

'Are you all right? Do you want anything else?' I asked my father when I went back to his room. He shook his head, his mouth full.

'She needs some more,' I told him.

'How much this time?'

'Just a few bob.'

He waved a knife at his coat and then dug it into his sausages.

I went through his pocket and felt notes at the bottom. Crunching a few into my hand I said, 'See you after Mass then,' and left the room quickly. I felt guilty and knew I'd have to go for a walk with him now.

After Mass we went up the mountains. We took our usual route along the mud track that bordered the fields avoiding the main road. We moved slowly, breathing heavily as each field rose steeper than the last.

'We're out of practice,' my father gasped, leaning on his stick and levering himself up with each step. Halfway up we stopped to look back.

'Look at them.' He pointed to a stream of tiny cars winding up the thin ribbon of road. 'They don't know what they're missing locked inside in their cars.' He threw back his head. 'Breathe deeply, Mar, and look up at the sun. Try and catch a sneeze.'

He was convinced this did wonders for your health.

I went through the motions but nothing happened. The sun was too weak and watery. He offered me his arm. 'D'you want to link?'

'No thanks.'

He swiped at a stone with his stick but it was lodged in the earth. 'About this school business, Marian. It seems a bit drastic living away from home. I hope you've made the right decision.'

I told him I had, but he went on.

'All that reading you've been doing. It's not like they say in books you know. Real life is different.'

'I know,' I said and quickened my step, annoyed he thought books had anything to do with it.

He caught up with me. 'But if it's what you want I won't say another word. Just learn all you can while you're there. I don't know how long the funds will last. This Hire Purchase business is killing me. But I have to keep up with the big stores. Did I tell you Arnotts made me another offer? They must be getting desperate but don't let on to your mother.'

Arnotts was one of the biggest stores in Dublin. They backed on to my father's shop. When they'd wanted to expand he'd objected saying the new building would block all the light from his office. They offered compensation but he refused. My mother nearly went mad. 'But that hole of yours is so dark the lights have to be kept on winter and summer. Think what a difference a lump sum would make.' But he wouldn't listen.

'Are you tempted?' I asked.

'Not at all.' He swished the grass with his stick and began to whistle.

The roar of the river reached us before we came to the bridge. We stood in the centre and watched the water hurtling below our feet.

'D'you remember the races we used to have?' He took an empty matchbox from his pocket and offered it. I chose the lid and smiled. He must have saved it specially I thought.

'Are you right?' He gave the signal. We dropped the two halves into the water. They shot off together. I chased after them along the bank and felt the old excitement coming back. When they got tangled up in weeds I yelled for mine to come on. It broke free and rejoined the current. I cheered as it raced on towards the falls before plunging into the torrent below.

'You won.' My father came up smiling and gave me a hug. I pulled away and looked at my watch.

'We can't go back yet, Mar, we haven't reached the gap. Come on, I'll give you a hand.' He linked my arm through his and we trudged on. His favourite view was from the gap at the top where you could look down over the city of Dublin.

I hadn't noticed the sun go in. A mist came up, encircling us like smoke. Everything looked bleak. The few trees that grew there were all stunted and bent from the constant wind that prematurely aged them.

There was no sign of the city when we reached the gap, it had vanished in the mist.

'What a shame, you can't see a thing.' My father turned to me.

The air felt thick, it was difficult to breathe. I tugged on his arm. 'Let's go, we've made it to the top.' I turned my hood up. The mist had grown heavy, beading our coats with soft rain.

'Don't worry.' He patted my arm. 'We'll be back in no time, it's downhill from now on.'

*   *   *

32

On the way home he stopped off at a pub pretending he had to go to the Gents but it was just an excuse for a drink. I walked on slowly hoping he'd catch up.

The smell of roast hit me at the gate. Don't say they haven't eaten yet, I thought, when I saw my mother straining something in the sink. Clouds of steam billowed around her and ran in streaks down the windows and walls.

'My feet are frozen,' she complained when she saw me, 'but I have to keep the door open. The condensation is dreadful.' I edged past her. She was always moaning about spending half her life in a poky kitchen standing on a stone floor. She was convinced the man who built it must have hated women. 'You're back early, what's happened to your Daddy?' She shook the colander vigorously.

'He got talking to someone along the road.'

'Well, he'd better hurry up, I'm just about to lift the dinner.' She handed me a bunch of cutlery. 'Here, take these in quick, that one's waiting on her dinner. She's driven me demented all morning and to cap it all Chard never rang.'

Celine sat with her head in her hands staring out the window. Napkins folded in peaks stood like sentries round the table. I said excuse me, but she wouldn't budge when I tried to set her place. My father suddenly appeared rubbing his hands.

'Nothing like a stiff walk to give you an appetite,' he beamed and sat down.

Celine's nose arched suspiciously. 'You've been drinking,' she said.

'Only enough to wet the whistle.' He gave me a wink and tucked a napkin under his chin.

My mother came in with the dinner. My father gave her a big smile. 'That looks good, Kitty, did anyone ever tell you you're a great cook?'

'Eat it while it's hot,' she said ignoring the smile.

My father began to eat. At each mouthful the back legs of his chair left the floor and fell back with a thud as he chewed noisily. His teeth, unable to keep up with his jaws, clicked like a crab gasping for water.

'This is my last Sunday dinner,' I said, trying to cover the sound.

'How absolutely fascinating, tell us more,' Celine sneered.

She picked a lettuce leaf out of her gravy and glared at my mother. 'One never serves lettuce on the same plate as a roast.'

'There's plenty more, dear, newly washed, do you want some?'

My father put down his knife and wrestled with a lump of gristle stuck between his teeth.

'Really, do you have to? It's absolutely disgusting.' Celine pushed her plate away. 'I'm not hungry.'

'How about some salad on a nice cold plate?' urged my mother.

Celine accepted with a pout and poked it listlessly with her fork. She stopped suddenly and stared in disbelief. We watched in horror as a tiny snail glided across her plate leaving a glistening trail in its wake. Celine's chair shot backwards. 'You did it on purpose,' she shouted at my mother.

My father suddenly lurched to his feet and grabbed the corners of the tablecloth. 'If you don't shut your mouth I'll pitch the whole damn lot through the window.'

I caught hold of his arm and begged him not to,

thinking of the mess. Celine started screaming and left the room slamming the door behind her. My mother daintily removed the napkin from her mouth and continued to eat. I eased my father back into his chair, wondering what made him fight back this time. He let go of the cloth and sat down looking pale.

I left them and went out to the garden. The light was fading and the sky was full of rain. I climbed up the beech tree and crouched there waiting. A bird squawked and flapped awkwardly away, scattering the uneven drops dripping from the branches. Pins and needles stole through my legs and settled into a steady cramp. I encouraged it by not moving. Lights beamed out from nearby houses, curtains were drawn against the night. Our house stood alone in darkness. I thought of the three of them locked away in their separate rooms.

The cramp grew worse and moved up to my waist. A light flashed in my father's room, off and on, two shorts and a long. Our special signal to call me home. He hated roaring my name around the neighbourhood the way other parents did. This time I was too numb to answer.

Chapter 5

Mellon's taxi was ordered for four. It arrived on time but my mother wasn't ready. She was still in her dressing gown dosing herself with Bisodol in case she got hot flushes on the way. When Mellon loaded up the trunk she got into a panic and sent me out to keep him talking till she was ready.

Mellon ignored children. He'd so many of his own I was never sure if it was twelve or fourteen since the birth of the twins. He looked exactly like his son Rusty. They'd the same ferret look and carrot-coloured hair. We'd been in Infants together. On our first day a huge dark figure in the toilet frightened me so much I peed instead on the classroom floor. When everyone sniggered and pointed at the puddle, I pointed at Rusty.

'How's Rusty?' I asked Mellon.

'Who?' He looked blank.

'Your son, Rusty.'

'Oh aye, him,' he said and stabbed his cigarette out on the dashboard. The smoke dissolved slowly in silence and I was relieved when my mother came out. The car rocked as she got in.

'I'm sorry to have kept you, Mr Mellon, but there's so much going on in our house, I don't know if I'm coming or going.'

She struggled forward and offered him a cigarette.

37

'No thanks, missus. I've just quenched one.' The car started up. I turned for a last look. Our house seemed brown and faded through the tinted window like an old photograph.

'What school did you say it was?' Mellon asked my mother.

'Loreto Abbey. Do you know it at all, Mr Mellon? It's a lovely place set in its own grounds.'

'It's not the Loreto Abbey,' I interrupted her. 'It's Loreto Abbey Dalkey. Loreto Abbey is the mother school and much more expensive.'

'Well, they still know how to charge.' She nudged with her foot and gave me a look. 'D'you know how much it's going to set us back, Mr Mellon?' He didn't answer, but she went on and told him the price anyway. Then she started telling him about Celine and the fortune teller she'd consulted about her future.

I leant my head against the window and felt it vibrate. The car was going fast, we'd get there too soon. My father was distant when he said goodbye, and just urged me to learn all I could as it was paid for.

We belted along the coast road. The tide was miles out practically touching the horizon. I kept my eye on it, as it felt comforting somehow, but then it kept disappearing behind hedges and buildings.

'Promise me for my sake, will you, Marian?' My mother turned to me questioningly.

'What?' I asked.

'That you'll offer up your prayers for Celine's success and maybe you'd ask the nuns to pray for her as well?'

'I will,' I said to shut her up. We'd entered a narrow road with granite walls on either side like the ones round the asylum. We edged through a pair of gates with the letters LAD cut deeply into a stone arch. The school was built like a castle with turrets and slit windows encased behind iron bars. A huge cross, starkly outlined against the sea, stood in the centre of a flowerbed. The black figure of a nun knelt before it. The car stopped. My mother got out and rang the bell.

Mellon darted a quick look at the nun and said to me in a low voice: 'I don't envy you.'

Another nun came to greet us. She wore a long flowing habit. A starched white headdress framed her face and came down over her chest like a bib. Rosary beads and a heavy crucifix hung from her waist. After she shook hands with my mother they disappeared under her bib.

'So this is Marian.' She smiled and nodded.

'Yes, Sister. I've just the two. Marian's the younger.'

'Now you mustn't worry, Mrs O'Dea, she'll soon settle down.'

'I'm sure she will, Sister, and you won't forget to pray for Celine will you, Marian? Celine's my eldest you see, Sister . . .'

My mother went on telling the nun about Celine and the Record Cup and how important it was. The nun kept smiling and nodding. She reminded me of the statue of Blessed Martin de Porres who stood on top of the poor box and nodded every time you dropped a penny in.

When my mother finished the nun asked if she'd like to pay a visit to the chapel.

'We're storming heaven with prayers for peace at the moment,' she added.

'Not today, thank you, Sister, I must be getting back, and there's Mellon, I can't keep him waiting. You know how men are.'

They exchanged knowing smiles. My mother held her cheek out to be kissed.

'Now be good, Marian, and do everything the nuns tell you.' She got into the car, the door slammed, the wheels crunched away over the gravel and they were gone.

The nun took a watch from the folds of her habit. 'Let me see, it's the study period now. I'd better take you to the dormitory.' She led the way into the convent through several immaculately clean rooms. The floors were so shiny I thought they must be wet. On the wall of one room a framed notice read:

CHILDREN OF QUALITY DO NOT
LINGER LONG IN WOOLWORTHS

We passed a doorway, and the nun went down on one knee. She blessed herself and looked up at me inquiringly. I knelt and did the same, noticing the dimly lit chapel through the glazed panel with just the glow of the Perpetual Light hanging before the altar.

We set off briskly down a long corridor. A nun wearing an apron gave us a wan smile and continued sprinkling what looked like tea leaves behind the hot pipes. She was a lay Sister. They did all the hard work and could never become Mothers because they were too poor to bring a dowry when they entered the convent.

We went up a stone staircase, the nun pointing out things on the way. Over an archway leading to the toilets hung a replica of the cloth Veronica used to wipe Christ's face. The image, etched in blood with sunken eye sockets, gave me the creeps. The corridor leading to the dormitory was lined with the Stations of the Cross. Endless pictures of Christ dragging his cross up Calvary. The last one showed him crucified. Jesus, I thought, imagine having to pass this lot on your way for a pee in the middle of the night.

'This is your dormitory,' the nun said, throwing open a door marked St Rochs. She told me to find a cubicle with my name on it and she'd send a child to tell me what to do.

The dormitory, lined with iron beds, had windows on one side facing the sea. I found my name on one against the wall and looked with envy at the window beds. It was almost dark outside. Far out to sea little points of light gleamed on and off as if answering each other in the night. A scraping noise outside the door made me freeze. Something heavy was being dragged along the floor. The door opened and a nun in an apron appeared pulling something behind her. When I saw it was my trunk I rushed to help. We carried it to the bed. One of her shoulders was higher than the other and gave her a hunted look. She smiled when I thanked her and left without a word. Maybe she's deaf, I thought. All the maids at Owen's school were deaf mutes. He said they were amazing, you could do anything to them and they never uttered a word.

A bell rang. I started to unpack wondering how I'd fit everything into the tiny locker beside my bed. A stampede of footsteps in the corridor outside made me stop. They faded away. Then I noticed a girl in the doorway with a great beam on her face. I learnt later her name was Mags and she always entered a room like that. It made people take notice. She'd read it somewhere and urged me to do the same.

'Hi,' she said. 'Why did you get sent here?'

'No reason. I wanted to come.'

'You must be nuts.' She sat down on the bed and began folding my clothes into neat piles.

'Why did you come then?' I asked.

'Had to. My old man begged me. He was going off his head. First my mother died, then my brother ran into a brick wall on his motorbike. Then an aunt came to live with us and got a brain haemorrhage. Our car could find its own way to the cemetery. We've made a deal though. He promised to let me leave after my Inter.'

I wanted to say how sorry I was but she was looking hopefully into my food bag. I took out the peanut butter, bottle of vinegar and cucumber my mother had packed.

'Thanks. You can't keep food here. You're supposed to take it to the refectory and share it out.' She opened the peanut butter and scooped out a lump.

'What's it like here?' I asked.

'Desperate. You're half starved and spend most of the time on your knees. And those bells. Jesus! There's one to get up, one to go downstairs, one for Mass and morning prayers, one to start eating, another to stop, one to leave the refectory . . .'

I stopped listening. She looked so grown up, with a bust and her hair cut short in a modern style.

'Better leave one out.' She nodded to the hankies I was stacking in the locker. 'Most people cry themselves to sleep the first night and you look the type. We've been back three weeks now and the country ones are still at it. They're right drips. Still, you can't blame them, they live so far from home and don't get many visits.'

A bell rang louder than the last making us jump.

'Have to go. They're coming up.'

'Don't you sleep here?' I asked.

'No, I'm in Holy Angels.' She gave me a wink and was gone.

The footsteps returned. I drew the curtains round my bed and watched through a chink as the door burst open and girls all shapes and sizes trooped in. In their navy tunics and black stockings they looked like orphans. Curtains were drawn, some queued at the sink, no one spoke. I undressed quickly and got into bed. A nun's voice began, 'Out of the depths I have cried to thee, O Lord. Lord hear my voice . . .'

Everyone responded in a singsong voice:

'Tower of Ivory

'Pray for us

'House of Gold

'Pray for us

'Ark of the Covenant

'Pray for us

'Gate of Heaven

'Pray for us

'Morning star

'Pray for us.'

I lay in bed thinking how strange it seemed to be asking a house of gold or a morning star to pray for you, when the curtains were suddenly pulled back. A nun stood there frowning.

'It is the custom in this school to address God on our knees and not from the comfort of one's bed.'

I slid out on to the floor and turned red. She went away leaving the curtains apart.

After prayers, beds creaked and lights went off. I inched the curtains closed and listened to the silence until somebody coughed. That started up a whole series of coughing till the nun snapped: 'We will dispense with the usual airing of lungs. As I've told you before, coughing is an affectation and quite unnecessary.'

A bed creaked muffling a cough. Someone giggled. I

heard sniffling from the next cubicle, and beyond the faint roar of the sea. I thought of my family at home. They seemed light years away, on another planet.

Mags was wrong. I didn't need the handkerchief.

Chapter 6

Next morning a loud bell crashed through my dreams and lights went on. I fell out of bed stunned by the noise not quite knowing where I was. A nun came round chanting 'Benedicamus Domino'. Everyone answered 'Deo Gratias', as a dish of holy water was thrust through the curtain.

While we made our beds the girl in the next cubicle who'd been crying during the night gave me a mournful smile. Her dark red gums almost covered her teeth, a startling contrast against her white face.

Another bell sent us hurrying downstairs to a honey-combed press for our missals and veils. A nun called Mother Borgia eyed us suspiciously as we bowed our way past her into the chapel.

The young priest took hours to say Mass. In the middle of it the sun streamed through the stained-glass windows throwing beams of coloured light over everyone. Mags, who was sitting in front, turned to me and smiled. Maybe it won't be so bad, I thought.

After Mass, all the nuns left but we had to stay on for morning prayers. Halfway through, the smell of rashers drifting through the chapel reminded me of how hungry I was.

At breakfast a nun walked up and down reading about self-mortification. The sisters carried in huge pots of tea. There was no sign of any rashers. Just dull-looking bread and marmalade. The top slices had curled and everyone avoided them. When the bell rang everyone started talking. The girl next to me had carefully divided her butterpat into four.

'You only get one,' she explained when I asked her why. Her name was Dunla and she'd history dates written on the backs of her hands.

'D'you play hockey?' a large blonde girl asked. I nodded, not wanting to let on I was terrified of the ball which I was sure could kill you if it got you in the head.

'I'm Columba, Captain of Games,' she said, squeezing my hand. Then the bell rang and we had to keep quiet.

There was a timetable for every minute of the day. Mags thought it a dead bore, but it was a relief for me to know what to do from one day to the next and that Celine couldn't barge in and create a scene.

When the day pupils came in after breakfast it was like ordinary school. They were our only contact with the outside world and decent about posting letters and bringing in food. We were never allowed out, except to play matches and even then a coach took us directly there and back. To get on a team you had to do rounds, that meant running round the hockey field at least ten times.

The first time, I got so winded after only two I slipped away down the field to where two giant rocks, balanced on top of each other, stuck out of the ground. Crouched beneath on the other side was Mags.

'Get down, for Christ's sake.' She waved me to her side.

'Aren't you afraid they'll fall?' I eyed the rocks anxiously.

'Nah, I tried to shift them once when Mother Borgia was passing but they wouldn't budge.'

I smiled but she didn't seem to be joking. We heard voices panting in the distance.

'Sssssssssch.' Mags put a finger to her mouth. 'They're only on their fourth.' We sat quietly staring out over a turquoise sea tinged with foam. Dark patches of sea-weed like winding roads ran through it in all directions. A little island with a ruin lay to the right.

'That's Dalkey Island where monks lived once,' Mags whispered, following my eyes. She pointed out a narrow lane running down to the sea. 'There's a tunnel down by the rocks that used to go all the way out to the island. It's supposed to be haunted.'

'Why?' I whispered, suddenly feeling creepy.

'There was this nun who'd a crush on one of the monks. They used to meet halfway.' She beamed. 'Imagine doing it with a monk under the sea?'

I couldn't but smiled anyway.

'One day the tunnel collapsed as they were on their way to meet each other. They say it was the hand of God.'

'What happened?'

'He swam to the surface and got away but her body was never found. She's supposed to be still out there waiting.'

I shivered suddenly; she laughed.

'You're dead,' a voice came from above.

We looked up and saw Columba on the rocks.

'Just because you're Captain doesn't mean you're God,' Mags called to her.

With a piercing cry Columba jumped off the rocks and landed between us. Mags shrieked and rolled away. I laughed, but Columba turned on me angrily and asked

47

if I'd special leave not to do rounds? I walked away and heard her voice grow warm as she told Mags she'd her name down as a sub to play Foxrock next Saturday.

Visitors were allowed in the parlour on Sundays. My father came the first Sunday and never missed a week after that. He always brought sandwiches cut from the roast and kept them in his breast pocket. Next to his heart to keep them warm, he said.

One weekend as we sat looking out to sea he watched me wolf them down. 'They must be starving you here. How long d'you think you'll stick it?'

'But I've only just come. What about all the expense?' I said, annoyed with him for not taking it more seriously.

'Damn the expense if you're not happy.'

'But I have to go to school.'

'I left at fourteen and it didn't do me any harm.'

'But you're not me and that was ages ago.'

'Ah, come on, Mar, let's not fight, time's too short.' He took my arm and smiled but his face looked drawn in the piercing wind.

That Sunday we'd a match and they needed a centre half.

'D'you have to go?' my father asked, looking at his watch.

'No, but I'd like to.' I slipped my hand through his and gave it a squeeze.

'But I've only just come.'

'I know, I'm sorry, but I can't let them down.'

'You know your old home town is lonely without you,' he said as we hugged goodbye.

'You'd think I'd moved to foreign parts,' I joked.

'That's what it feels like,' he said and walked away

looking so down my eyes filled up till he went through the gate.

The girls teased me later with, 'Who's the boyfriend?' because he looked mysterious in his long black coat and we walked round arms linked. Mags thought it crazy to be going round with my father like that at my age.

Although I knew they were only kidding, something like that happened before when my father took me to the Gaiety. We were holding hands during the show when these creeps behind started calling him names like Sugar Daddy and Lover Boy. My father got up in a rage and reported them to the manager demanding they be thrown out. The manager was reluctant as it was the middle of the show and a full house. He asked me was it really that bad? I said no to avoid any more embarrassment. He offered us seats for another night, but my father refused and we went home miserable.

Chapter 7

Mother Borgia stopped me in the corridor one day to say she admired the picture of Swan Lake I'd hung over my bed but wondered was it suitable, especially during Lent. She advised me to take it down and she'd give me a picture of the Blessed Virgin instead. The same thing happened to another girl with her picture of Richard Burton as a centurion. She pretended it was her brother but Mother Borgia said she hadn't been in the convent that long to know it wasn't and took it away from her.

Mother Borgia said she hoped I was settling in and working hard in order to repay my parents for the sacrifices they'd made to send me here. Then she started talking about school traditions and guarding against bad influences. I stopped listening and wondered what her hair looked like behind the stiff headdress that framed her long narrow face. Loose, curly hair would do a lot to soften it, but nothing could be done for the thin mouth that drooped downwards. She'd stopped talking and was eyeing me questioningly. 'There must be something you wish to know or are unsure of?' she urged briskly. I stared back blankly feeling a fool in the silence. All I wanted to know about were the facts of life. I'd asked Mags, who couldn't believe I was so ignorant and told me it was all in the first half of the

Hail Mary. I said it over and over again but couldn't find anything.

> Hail Mary full of grace, the Lord is with thee,
> Blessed art thou amongst women
> And Blessed is the fruit of thy womb Jesus.

I thought there might be something in the words 'with thee'.

If someone was with you what could they be doing? I moved on to the next line, 'Blessed art thou amongst women'. When I was a kid I always thought the words were 'blessed art thou a monk swimming', from the way people gabbled through the Rosary. But now that I knew the exact words it still didn't mean anything.

The last line, 'Blessed is the fruit of thy womb Jesus', was more promising. Fruit of thy womb obviously meant you'd a baby inside you, but it didn't explain how it got there. I was back where I started and still didn't have a clue.

'D'you know now?' Mags asked later. I nodded. 'And to think, you must have said the Hail Mary millions of times and it's never clicked until now?'

'I know,' I said absolutely convinced I was a hundred per cent dumb.

I decided to take the plunge now with Mother Borgia. 'It's about the facts of life . . .' I began hesitantly.

She glanced down the corridor and drew us closer into the alcove window draped in heavy brown curtains.

'Have you spoken to your mother or anyone else about this?'

I shook my head. My mother never even told us about our periods. When Celine got hers she thought she was dying and got into a cold bath to stop the flow. After that whenever I made the beds I always knew her time of the month. In the same way, when I saw stains on my father's sheets I thought men must have white periods, but more often.

'It's all very simple,' Mother Borgia said. 'Although not strictly necessary until you leave home or go on to university.'

'Maybe I'll wait then,' I said, feeling a sudden urge to get away.

'No, well begun is half done and careless talk can lead to more serious sins.' She tossed her habit away from her face and began talking rapidly about flowers and pollen which made no sense at all. It sounded so boring I wondered what it had to do with the monk and nun doing it? All I could think of was the time I stayed in Owen's caravan in Portmarnock and woke during the night to hear his parents arguing. His father was begging his mother for something and she kept saying no. In the end she gave in if he promised to take the whole family to Ibiza. It went quiet for a bit, but then the caravan started shaking and he was gasping and moaning. It sounded desperate and next morning she smelt queer in her nightgown.

'Now do you understand?' Mother Borgia asked when she'd finished.

'Yes,' I lied anxious to get away.

Chapter 8

Once the day pupils went home we'd study till bedtime with breaks for prayers, tea and recreation.

Recreation was held in the concert hall. Apart from table tennis there was nothing to do except foxtrot to some Glenn Millers. Columba danced with Mags; it was more of a walk. She led her solemnly till the music reached a climax then, swinging her roughly, whirled round and round till they ended in a heap on the floor. She only dared to do it when the old nuns were in charge. Mags said they were sent here as a last resort in the hope the sea air would put some life into them. You could get away with murder when they were on study. But not with Mother Borgia. She sat on the throne fingering her beads, and controlled the whole school with her eyes. They'd dart about looking for trouble, then slowly her neck would follow. Whenever her eyes landed on Dunla they softened and her mouth straightened out, the nearest she ever got to a smile. Dunla always sat in front with her fingers in her ears, swaying as she memorised facts.

'It's her only asset, leave her at it,' Mags said. But I'd this terrible urge to torment her, when I really should have felt sorry for her. She was covered in spots and had a slab cake kind of face you felt like slicing.

One night old Mother Gerard was in charge of the

study period. She couldn't see beyond the first two rows. Outside, the gulls had come in to land as a curtain of fog descended over the sea. They wheeled past the window silently. I felt safe at my desk by the window and was settling down to a Georgette Heyer smuggled from the library, when a knock came to the door. It was a parlour Sister to say I was wanted there. Something's wrong, I thought, as I put my book away and bowed to Mother Gerard. Visitors weren't allowed on weekdays.

The parlour was almost dark. I could barely make out the figure of my mother seated at the window. She seemed smaller somehow, her feet barely touching the ground. Clutching her handbag she looked anxious behind her glasses.

'What's up?' I asked.

'Oh, Marian, I had to come! It's dreadful at home. You've no idea, I can't do anything right. Celine's at me all the time. It's got that bad I'm afraid to open my mouth.'

A familiar weight grew in the pit of my stomach as I realised she'd only come to moan.

'I thought she'd won the Record Cup?'

'She did, but that was ages ago. Didn't your Daddy tell you all about it?'

I nodded.

'After she won, Gertie's phone never stopped ringing. Her picture was in all the papers. There was a queue of boys wanting to take her out. Poor Chard,' my mother beamed, 'he's had to put up with so much from her.'

'So it hasn't made her any happier?' I said.

'Happier?' My mother looked puzzled. 'What's that got to do with it?'

To change the subject I asked how my father was.

'Don't mention him, he has driven me demented since you left. He's threatened to come out and bring you home a dozen times. I've had to restrain him. He's lost now without someone to go out with.'

'Well, why don't you go out with him?'

'Me?' She looked surprised.

'You're his wife. Why do the two of you never go out together?'

'Oh Marian, don't be annoying me,' she sighed. 'Haven't I enough on my plate with Celine. Anyway your father's never there. He's always in that shop of his working.'

'No he's not, he goes out with me, you've said so yourself, anyway you're always out at your Mothers' Guild, Whist Drives, trips to Lough Derg and God knows what else . . .' I trailed off as Mother Borgia swept into the room.

'What have we here?' she said and turned on the lights.

My mother struggled to her feet. I gave her a hand and introduced them.

'Hello, Sister,' my mother smiled, 'pleased to meet you.' They shook hands. 'I hope Marian's doing well?'

'It's early days,' Mother Borgia said sternly. 'I expect she's been telling you all about our life here. But may I remind you that visits are only allowed on Sundays between twelve and six.'

'I didn't realise,' my mother apologised.

'We'll overlook it this once. It's understandable I suppose, mother and daughter separated for the first time. You must have a lot of catching up to do so I won't detain you.'

She turned to me and her smile disappeared.

'Now remember, Marian. Prayers in chapel at six sharp.'

'Don't think much of that Sister,' my mother said when she left. She sat down with a sigh.

'She's not a Sister, she's Mistress of Studies, all the teaching nuns are called Mothers.'

'For God's sake, what does it matter?'

'But only the lay nuns are called Sisters . . .' I tried to explain but she cut me off irritably.

'I can't do anything right can I? Would you leave me alone for God's sake, I wish I'd never come.' She sulked in silence till the sound of the clock striking reminded her that time was short.

'Where was I?'

I asked again about my father.

'Did he tell you Celine got a job in the Gate?'

I shook my head.

'She turned her nose up at it first. "Me, a wardrobe assistant, mending other people's clothes?" Between you and me, Marian, she can't even thread a needle. But I told her take it, Celine, you'd be a fool not to, it can only lead to bigger things. There was even a mention of juvenile leads at the interview. And she's in a play already, it opened last week. It's a thriller I believe, but she won't let me go and see it yet. Look, she even got a mention in the paper.' Opening her bag she carefully unfolded a newspaper cutting from the leaves of her prayer book and read: "A chill of fear ran through the audience at the Gate Theatre last night causing some of its members to rise from their seats as Lennox Robinson's new play, 'Ill Met by Moonlight', reached its thrilling climax. I am not going to spoil the plot by revealing the ending . . ."'

My mother smiled and put the piece away.

'But there's no mention of Celine?' I said.

'There is, that's where she comes in.'

'Where?'

'As a shadow.'

'A what?'

'A shadow on the wall and to think she had them on their feet. Everyone's flocking to see it. There'll be no stopping her now. It's a great start.'

To shut her up about Celine, I asked again about my father.

'It's a great pity you kept him out in the grounds last Sunday when he came to see you. He said he never felt so cold. A grand excuse for a drink. He came home stocious. I don't know what's got into him lately, any excuse and he's off on a binge. Luckily I got him up to bed before Celine arrived home with her theatrical friends.'

I was going to tell her he'd left early because of the hockey match, but thought better not.

She smiled. 'You know there's no holding her now since she joined the Gate. Though she nearly wiped the floor with me one night. She gave me strict instructions to prepare a big bowl of rice, and I made it just right, eggs, cream, not too much sugar, and a dash of nutmeg. You should have seen her face when she opened the oven door. You fool, she said and flung it across the floor. All that lovely rice and my best Pyrex smashed to smithereens. How was I to know she was going to bring back some curry thing, never even heard of it.'

'What did her friends think?'

'Oh, she passed it off with her usual flair. Said she'd dropped the rice and they'd have to eat out. They went off laughing. D'you know your Daddy had the audacity to call down and ask what the commotion was. Said he couldn't sleep with all the racket. But I soon shut him up.'

I couldn't bear to hear any more and watched with relief the hands of the parlour clock inch towards six.

'It's time for prayers,' I said, getting up.

'Oh, I know when I'm not wanted.' She gathered up her things in a huff.

'No really, it's the rules.' I followed her outside where the mist had turned to a steady rain.

'Would you look at the night that's in it, you can't see a hand in front of you,' she complained.

A foghorn boomed, startling us. She bunched her coat up round her neck and shivered. 'Just listen to that, it'd put years on you.'

She offered me her cheek. ''Bye, dear, I'll write and let you know how things are. Oh, I nearly forgot, we're getting a phone at last. Celine's been tormenting your Daddy for ages. He only agreed so he can keep in touch now that you're away.'

Her footsteps crunched on the gravel as she headed for the gate. ''Bye,' I called out, but my voice never reached her and there was no reply.

Chapter 9

A rumour was going round that something awful had been found and Mother Borgia called a meeting for seniors only in the concert hall.

Looking very grave she told us that objectionable internal tampons used during the monthly cycle had been found in the day pupils' toilet. She warned us against them, as Irish Catholic doctors not only considered them undesirable, but discovered that unhealthy discharges occurred in certain cases after using them.

Mother Borgia told us that they were strictly forbidden, and the only ones permitted were pads which were tied or pinned on, and never the kind which had to be inserted.

I hadn't a clue what she was on about and asked Mags. Columba overheard and said I was as thick as ten folds in a blanket. But Mags said she'd a book about these things an aunt sent from England and she'd bring it back with her after the break.

We were allowed home for a few days before the exams. My father came to collect me in Mellon's taxi and I persuaded him to give Mags a lift home as well. She'd invited me to stay at her place, as her father, a builder, was away a lot down the country. She'd a brother in Alaska. Another lived at home but spent most of his time in bed reading. Mags said he never wore pyjama bottoms. Once, for laughs, a friend and herself tried to drag him out of bed but he was really strong. They struggled for ages, but he was able to fend them off even with one hand clutching the covers.

In the car Mags kept calling her father her old man, which really annoyed my father. Then she went on about all the deaths in her family and how she could do with a bit of company and it'd be great if I could stay, even for a night. 'We'll see,' my father said when we dropped her off which meant no.

For once my mother opened the door smiling. But then Celine was doing well she said as she took my coat. It seemed that Celine was staying with the Bouchier-Haweses, hopefully her future in-laws. Not only that, but the latest present from Chard got my mother all excited. It was a tiny gold wristwatch. She was convinced a ring would follow if Celine played her cards right, and thought a pilgrimage to Lough Derg might help things along.

The dining room looked cosy with the fire lit and the table set for three with my mother's home baking. It would have been perfect if I hadn't spoilt it for some reason by trying to start a row with my father.

What was wrong with Mags? Why didn't he like her? She was my best friend and I'd stay with her if I wanted to.

This was stupid really. I knew if I stayed with Mags I'd have to ask her back to my house which was impossible. My father tried to joke me out of it.

'It's because you're sitting in that chair. Amn't I right, Kitty?' He smiled and turned to my mother, but she was engrossed in her tea and a pamphlet about Lough Derg.

'What are you talking about?' I asked him irritably.

'Don't you see? You're sitting in Celine's chair, and anyone who sits there acts like her.' He laughed, but I didn't think it funny and refused to join in.

My mother woke me early next morning and said she was off to Lough Derg.

'I've arranged for you to stay at Gertie's for the day,' she announced when I went down to the kitchen in a daze. She was buttering a heap of bread and refused to listen when I said I was well able to look after myself.

'Oh no you're not. There's another lunatic on the run,' she said handing me a flask to rinse out.

'Since when?'

'Night before last.'

'He must be miles away by now.'

'He's not, and since you're so persistent I may as well tell you he's been spotted in the old graveyard up a tree, stark naked. And to think,' she paused as she sliced the ham, 'that he passed down the road in the dead of night and I out hanging clothes on the line.' She shivered and, picking a sliver of meat up with the point of the knife, slipped it in her mouth. 'I'll not sleep easy till he's caught.'

'Sure, they're always escaping.'

'I know, but this one's a pervert.'

'What's a pervert?'

'Never you mind.'

'That other one was clever the way he built that boat,' I said remembering back to what seemed like an age ago.

'Clever? Sure, they're all demented. Just hot water will do,' she nodded to the simmering kettle. 'I want to purge out my system.'

I filled her flask as she sawed the crusts off her sandwiches and wrapped them in greaseproof.

'There's a bottle of Californian Poppy on my dressing table to take round to Gertie. I've never known that one do anyone a favour without wanting something in return. She wants to borrow it, she says. Borrow my eye. I'll never see it again. That's the second one she's had off me. What does she do with it, drink it?'

'When are they moving?' I asked, thinking it'd be nice to have a look at their new house.

'It's all off. They backed out at the last minute. Gertie couldn't face the upkeep of it. I don't wonder. The last time I was in her house I was itching to get my hands on the lid of the bread bin. You've never seen anything like the filth of it. Even the soap in the kitchen was dirty. Didn't I tell you she'd never do it justice. At least, she knows her limitations.' My mother packed her bag with great satisfaction and, putting on her coat, asked me to wish her luck.

Gertie's house was clean enough, but not compared to the high standards in our house. Dirt was my mother's worst enemy. It was a crime to wear shoes in the house, you had to take them off at the door. She scrubbed and polished everything once a week and laid newspapers on the shiny lino floor to protect it. We skidded round till they were removed at the weekend and then the whole cycle began again.

She hated flies, especially bluebottles. She spotted some on the rashers in the grocers one day and complained to the owner.

'The flies have to live too you know, Mrs O'Dea,' he answered casually. She nearly had a fit and took her custom elsewhere although we'd been dealing there for years.

The bluebottles got their own back when we went

away on holidays. As usual she left the house spotless. But when we returned after the fortnight her bedroom was alive with them. They'd hatched out in the chimney while we were away. My mother nearly passed out. She knew the neighbours must have seen the state of the window and thought how dirty she was. So she told them that a bird had built its nest in the chimney and they couldn't get out.

Chapter 10

Gertie was in the kitchen staring out the window. She gave a start when she saw me and, removing a butt from her mouth, threw it out the door. 'Would you like a drink?' she asked, and got out glasses and a sherry bottle. 'Some squash?'

'No thanks.'

She poured herself a drink. 'So your mother got off all right? Did she make the half ten?'

I nodded and placed the perfume on the table.

She pushed it absent-mindedly aside and poured herself another. 'When is she due back?'

'I dunno, later sometime.'

'I've never been to Lough Derg myself. Can't see the point, going uphill on your knees. God knows life's uphill enough without that.' She drained the glass.

'It's in your bare feet,' I told her.

'Whatever.' She waved her hand and filling her glass to the brim knocked it back in a gulp. 'Still, every cripple has his own way of walking.' She pursed her lips revealing fine cracks round her mouth.

I asked her about Rowan and Owen. She said Owen was away with his father, did I want Rowan?

'Not if he's busy?'

'Busy?' She laughed derisively and left the room. I heard her call his name over and over again, it sounded like a cry of rage. I went into the garden feeling depressed.

Rowan came out wearing shorts. Although there was less than a year between them he looked much younger than his brother. He kept bobbing about, from one foot to the next, bouncing a ball.

'Are you still in shorts?' I asked.

'No, I'm in longers. It's just when I'm training.'

'For what?'

'Nothin', just training. I'm mad on sports.'

He went down on his hunkers still hopping the ball. I turned away wondering would he ever grow up.

'What'll we do?' he asked. I shrugged.

'How about going up the asylum for balls?'

'You go if you like. I've loads.'

Rowan jumped up as the ball bounced higher. He was taller than I, but looked really puny. His arms and legs stuck out like sticks. He caught the ball and asked, 'What're you looking at?'

'Not much,' I said unkindly. We stared. His eyes couldn't match mine, they were too weak, and yet I liked him. He was the kind you'd trust to hold your ice-cream without licking it. I felt mean and touched his arm. 'C'mon.'

'What?' He pulled away.

'Let's go up the cemetery.'

'Naw, that's creepy.'

'It's not, it's full of history. Anyway what else is there to do?'

He shrugged and pocketed his ball. We took the short-cut through the fields at the bottom of the garden. The wind blew fresh in our faces after the quiet suburban garden as we whooped up the hill till we reached the gate. The old cemetery stood at the top and meandered downwards to the newer section, where identical rows of white tombstones seemed to merge into the identical rows of white houses nestling at their feet. Glittering glass-domed flowers studded the well-tended graves and gave an unnatural colour to the place.

The old part was a wilderness. Briars and nettles clung to our clothes as we picked our way through the overgrown paths. A flock of crows rose up, cawing loudly, from the dark cypresses. The place was deserted. Cattle, grazing quietly, looked up curiously as we approached, their mouths munching without stopping.

'They say it tastes queer.'

'What?' Rowan snapped a branch off a tree and peeled away the bark.

'Graveyard milk. The milkman told me, he said he wouldn't touch it, it's tainted.'

'I suppose so. It's the same when they eat garlic. It comes out in the milk.' He slashed away at the nettles and walked on ahead. I stopped by some gravestones. They sagged together, leaning inwardly, propping each other up. Some had collapsed altogether and were stacked neatly against the wall. Vines grew undisturbed, creeping through the worn slabs, blotting out the inscriptions. I tore away the leaves and traced my fingers over the words but could only make out the date.

'Seventeen fifty-four,' I called out.

'Ssssshhhhhh.' Rowan came stumbling over the uneven ground. 'Don't shout. It doesn't seem right, and you're standing on someone's grave.' I moved aside and showed him the stone. He examined it, whistling at the date. 'C'mon over here,' he said, 'there's an old vault.'

I followed him to a small stone house. The door

had no handle. We peered through the spiky barred window. Part of the floor had sunk in.

'I can see bones.' I nudged Rowan.

He jumped. 'Where?' and cupping his hands over his eyes tried to see in the gloom. We heard a hoarse cough and spun round in fright, but there was nobody there.

'Look out behind you, run for your life,' I cried out and belted off down the hill. Cows skittered away as we raced past them. Rowan swooped by and flew on ahead. As we neared the gate, I skidded on a cowpat and sat down. Rowan had disappeared. I stood up carefully and examined my skirt. It was covered in cowshit. I walked back slowly, holding it at arm's length, hoping I wouldn't meet anyone.

Rowan stood behind his gate looking scared.

'Who was it, what happened?'

'Just a cow.'

'A cow?'

'Have you never heard one cough?'

He laughed but I showed him the state of my skirt and asked what to do as I didn't want his mother to see. He told me to hide in their shed and promised to go round to my house and get some clothes.

In the shed I took off my skirt as it was ruined and threw it behind a pile of coal. A cat appeared and rubbed against me with arched back. I shoved it away. Cats gave me the creeps. They'd no loyalty and always went to the best home that was offered them. Dogs were different, they'd stick with you till the end. Like Bill Sykes's dog in Oliver Twist. I used to think cats were females and dogs males when I was a kid.

I heard footsteps outside and crouched down. Gertie came into view with a basket of washing. The cat ran out to her and entwined itself between her legs as she pegged clothes on the line. She spoke to it in that strange voice people use with animals and babies and, picking it up, buried her face in its neck. Her hair matched the cat's fur.

'Does he want his din-dins then?' she said, and carried it back to the house.

When she'd gone I nipped out to the line and borrowed one of her aprons. It went round me twice and hung damply between my legs, but it was better than nothing.

Rowan arrived in a fluster. 'I couldn't get anything, your father's there. He's waving a knife, I think he's drunk.'

'That's impossible,' I said and my heart sank.

'He is, I tell you, and there's someone with him. I think it's Carville the chemist. His car's outside.'

'He's not drunk. That's only the voice he puts on when he's telling a story,' I lied.

Carville was standing at our front door. I wondered what he was doing unless he'd come about the bill. He greeted me with a smile. I smiled back feeling a fool, as I always had since the day I'd gone into his shop and asked him how much were his ninepenny combs.

'I brought your father back. It seems he's been out celebrating.' I didn't say anything, as my father only drank when somebody died. 'He's invited me to tea but I really must get back.' He picked his hat off the hallstand. 'Tell him thanks all the same.'

My father was in the kitchen crouched over the sink rinsing his hand. Steam poured from the kettle boiling furiously on the stove. Drops of blood ran across the floor to where the ham lay hacked to pieces on the table. I turned off the gas. I couldn't see any knife.

'Life's blood running away and what's it all for, what a waste,' muttered my father.

'What happened?' I asked going over to him.

He watched in a daze the water swirl around the sink blotched with his blood.

'I'm bleeding to death and no one gives a damn.' He turned towards me and lurched backwards. 'Nobody cares.'

I caught hold of him and edged him towards a chair.

'Sssshhhh now, let's have a look.' I examined his hand. A deep gash ran down between his thumb and forefinger. He pulled it away and waved it round.

'Where's everyone? The place is deserted.'

A trickle of blood ran up his sleeve. I found an old sheet and tore it in strips. 'Where's your mother? I'm starving with the hunger.'

'She's gone to Lough Derg.'

'What's she doing there? Not the penance bit again. Delving into the past. Can she never forget that whole business?'

He sounded bitter. I tied the bandage tightly wondering what he was talking about and gave him back his hand.

'All the misery that woman's been through with that blackguard getting her into trouble. And she believed to the end his promises to marry her. D'you know, Marian, he tried to drown her in a boat off Ireland's Eye only someone came along.' He turned to me, eyes wide with disbelief.

'What are you talking about?' I asked but he didn't hear.

'It was only then she saw the light. But it nearly killed her. She wasn't fit to live after it.'

'C'mon,' I said trying to get him upstairs before the others came back. He always pretended to be totally locked when my mother and Celine were there. That way he wouldn't have to listen to them giving out.

He ignored me and went on. 'It was the child dying that put the cap on it. Then she realised she needn't have married me after all.' He leaned forward and stared into space lost in misery.

It suddenly dawned on me what he was talking about. 'What child? Who d'you mean? Was that my brother?'

He wouldn't answer. Unable to sit still I went to get up but he pulled me back on the chair.

'Stay here and talk to me, Marian.'

'Who are you talking about?' I asked knowing now what he meant.

'Some shite in England.'

'Where were you?'

'It was before my time.'

I wanted to comfort him but I couldn't think of anything to say.

'So I kept my side of the bargain and look what happened,' he continued. 'I got left. After Celine she wouldn't let me near her. It's a miracle you came along. Doesn't she realise I've got feelings too?' He looked at me with such hurt in his eyes I had to turn away. 'The joke of it is she's stuck with me now.' He let out a desperate laugh and began to cough. Then fumbling with his handkerchief he blew his nose. I thought he was crying and couldn't have borne it if my mother or Celine had walked in just then.

As if reading my thoughts he said, 'You won't tell your mother about any of this, will you, Marian? Promise me it will be our secret. Anyway, she's a good woman underneath it all, and does her best.'

I was touched by his loyalty but it annoyed me as well. Why did he never say anything bad about her when she never stopped giving out about him?

'It'll be our secret, won't it,' he repeated. 'We can have our little secrets too, can't we, Marian?'

'I won't tell, I promise.'

I went to make tea with my brain in a whirl thinking about my pious mother and her endless trips to Lough Derg.

My father must have had whiskey on him, because he got out a bottle when my back was turned and drained what was left. I went to take the bottle away, anxious to get him upstairs. I knew his capacity, a few drinks and he was gone. I put my hands under his armpits to lift him up but he took hold of them and pressed them to his chest.

'You're the one, Mar. You're the only one I care for now.'

'C'mon, let's go,' I said shouldering him up.

He held on to me and felt Gertie's apron.

'God, what's that you've on, Marian, you're all wet?'

'It's nothing. I'll change upstairs.'

I tried to keep him on the move, but he lurched sideways, caught hold of the apron and dragged it down leaving me standing there in my underpants.

'Sorry about that,' he apologised, watching as I pulled it up quickly and tied it on.

We took the stairs one at a time. He leant against me and I clung to the banisters, terrified we'd be pitched headlong backwards. Upstairs, I kicked his bedroom door. It careered off the wall and bounced back as we staggered through. He sat heavily on the bed. I took his coat. Baby Powers clanked together in the pockets as I hung it in the wardrobe. I hid them behind a chair, knowing he'd be desperate for the cure in the morning. He turned clawing the buttons of his shirt.

'What's that you've done with my coat?'

'Just hanging it up.'

I took his pyjamas, neatly folded by my mother, from their starched case and helped him on with the jacket. He stood up and began to fumble with his trousers. I turned the bed down quickly and left the room. I was beginning to feel cold and changed into my dressing gown.

He was lying on the bed with his eyes shut when I returned. I tiptoed over to the window and gently drew the curtains. As I went to tuck him in, he opened his eyes. Then I saw his pyjama cord was undone, the fly gaped open. I looked up at his face and started. He was watching me quietly. Our eyes met and held. I waited, willing him to cover himself up. He seemed strangely sober now, as if waiting to see what I'd do. In spite of myself, I felt drawn to look down at him again. The room was deathly quiet. He didn't move. I reached towards him and swiftly took hold of the covers and pulled them firmly up to his chin. He turned aside quickly and pressed his face into the pillow. I heard a sob as I left the room.

Downstairs I listened but the house remained deathly still. A bluebottle buzzed giddily about before coming to rest somewhere. I closed the living room door and put on one of my records. Dusk had begun to settle outside. I sat by the window to watch. Ravel's *Bolero* thundered round the room, the theme repeating itself over and over again.

It blotted everything out in my head. Not to think was best. Not to think about anything. As the music grew more and more intense, I wondered could he hear it. Was he lying awake listening? What was he thinking about? Or was he thinking about anything? Would he even remember in the morning?

That night I had a dream. It was more of a nightmare, but not the usual kind. We were all drowning. The four of us, my father, mother, Celine and me. Thrown about by huge waves we tried desperately to cling on to each other, but it was no good. We kept being sucked down. Somehow my mother managed to get Celine on her back and, rising up on a wave, used my father and me as stepping stones to make her way to shore. Her teeth had fallen out and she was grinning ecstatically. The weight of her on top of us pushed us down further and my father and I, clasped together, turning over and over, sank slowly to the bottom.

I woke up, gasping for breath, but full of relief when I realised it was only a dream.

After that my father went on a binge for days. This surprised my mother as no one she knew of had died.

Chapter 11

A priest came to the convent to give a retreat before the exams. This meant silence for two days to contemplate God and examine our souls. We were free, though, to walk round the grounds praying or reading holy books. At first everyone looked as if they were praying madly with mouths moving feverishly, but it turned out they were studying textbooks covered in brown paper.

I found a great book on the lives of the Saints. My favourite, St Catherine, not only died on the wheel but offered her body to God as an anvil on which he could hammer the sins of the world. He took her at her word and used her body as a target for four months. After this ordeal, she was still able to walk unaided to receive His Body before falling into an ecstasy.

Another modern-day saint kept being tempted by the devil in different disguises. One day he cleverly took on the appearance of a telephone but she spotted him straight away and hurled him across the room.

Mags nicknamed the retreat priest Rubberlips, because they spread over his face whenever he smiled. He gave lectures in the afternoon. The one on Purity and Temptation was for senior girls only. He spoke joyfully of the precious jewel of purity bestowed on all Catholic girls and advised us to say a Hail Mary every night to keep this jewel shining and intact. Sometimes it could happen that a wrong or impure thought crept into our mind. So far, we could not be blamed. But once we realised it was there we were obliged under pain of mortal sin to blot it out. The best way to do this was to think of something else like stamp-collecting, games, or whatever caught our fancy.

In the middle of this the most divine smell of roast beef drifted through the chapel. The nuns had laid it on specially for the priest. Mags noticed it the same time as I did. We both breathed deeply, rubbed our stomachs and went 'Mmmmmm' together before dissolving into a fit of giggles. The prefects turned and gave us filthy looks. Luckily the nuns weren't there.

Celine paid a surprise visit. She arrived in a Morris Minor with a boy I'd never seen before. God help him, he was teaching her to drive. They got stuck coming through the gates and he had to take over. I'd been watching from the window, wondering who was getting a visit when I saw her jump out of the car and bang the door in a fury.

'Don't flatter yourself,' she sneered, 'I only came for the spin.'

The boy, skinny with glasses, had gone for a scout round by the time I got down to them. I asked who he was?

'No one in particular.' She shrugged and handed me a Tea Time Express cake sent by my father.

'Isn't he coming this week?' I asked.

She climbed into the driver's seat ignoring me. This probably meant he was still on the booze.

The cake was all squashed, but it didn't matter. It was my favourite, a jam pastry, with chocolate and almonds.

It smelt so good, I broke a piece off. Celine insisted on some; we ate in silence.

'Could Chard not teach you to drive?' I asked for something to say.

'Mind your own business,' she snapped and started the car. The engine roared.

'Are you off so soon? Don't you want a look round?' I parcelled the cake up quickly.

But she was bored already and beeped the horn impatiently till the boy came running up from the sea. He got in without a word and they lurched off. Another of her slaves, I thought, and didn't wait to see if they made it through the gate.

Mags was always going on about how much she wanted a sister so I told her a bit about Celine.

Pretend she's suffering from some incurable disease and it's her last day every time you see her, she advised.

That night I dreamt I was in a Roman amphitheatre and Celine was charging round in a chariot waving a whip like a conqueror. The only person in the audience was my mother, on her feet applauding triumphantly. Then I noticed Celine's chariot wasn't drawn by horses, instead she was lashing out at our father, Chard and the new boyfriend.

Next morning the dormitory nun gave me a lie on. She said I'd been sleepwalking during the night. She'd caught me just in time at the top of the stairs. It was bliss lying on while the others traipsed down to Mass. Mags always tried to get a lie on by stuffing blotting paper in her shoes. She thought the blood would rush to her feet and make her faint, but it never worked.

The exams were looming up. Every night the study

buzzed with rows of navy backs, heads down memorising facts. I tried to concentrate, but whenever I opened a book, yawns stifled me and my eyes drifted out to sea. Could do better if she tried, my past reports said. But I was trying now and nothing would sink in. My brain had gone blank.

In a panic I went over every subject and realised that English and Art were the only two I'd stand a chance in. Even Domestic Science, usually a cinch, hadn't worked out. The cookery bit was all right but not the sample buttonhole. At every attempt my thread got tangled up which made the buttonhole fray.

Mother Borgia had us for needlework. All through the exam she sat on the throne, reminding us at intervals how much time we'd left. Mags was brilliant at sewing and had finished already. The room relaxed as more work was laid down. In my hurry to finish I pulled hard on the needle, the material bunched up and shot out of my hand. Mother Borgia gave me a look and announced we'd four minutes left.

Flattening my buttonhole I tried again but the thread, limp from licking, refused the eye of the needle. Nearly everyone had finished by now and Mother Borgia asked Mags to bring up her work.

'Very good.' She nodded approvingly, and gave Mags ninety-eight per cent. Sighs of admiration went up but were cut short.

'Time's up. Will those who have not yet finished please put down their work.'

Mine was such a mess I tore at it savagely. Then, to top it all, the needle pierced my finger and I watched with satisfaction as specks of blood dotted the material finishing it off altogether. I signalled to Mags to lend me hers. She slipped it under the table. I went and joined the line. Mother Borgia took it with a look of derision and threw back her veil to examine it carefully. I winked at Mags.

'I suppose we'll give you forty per cent,' she said begrudgingly.

'Only forty?' I argued. 'But that's barely a pass, one mark less and I'd have failed.'

'Are you questioning my judgement, Marian O'Dea?'

It was so unfair I blurted out like a fool that it was Mags's work and she'd just given her ninety-eight out of a hundred for it.

The class went quiet as Mother Borgia stood up with a face like granite and ordered me out of her class for ever.

Chapter 12

A keen wind blew in from the sea gusting wildly as it reached the top of the hill where I lay. It was recreation time but the place was deserted. Everyone was in cramming for the Irish exam next day. If you failed Irish you automatically failed everything else.

Groaning at the thoughts of the History paper that morning I huddled into the grass and spotted a four-leafed clover which I stuck in my buttonhole for luck. The History exam went on for two and a half hours and was disastrous. Everyone wrote non-stop but I couldn't answer a thing. I spent ages ruling my paper with perfect margins, date, title, class and name all in order. The one question I attempted – 'Who was Red Hugh O'Donnell?' – dried up before it even reached the end of the line. I wrote:

'Red Hugh O'Donnell was a—' and that's all, but I had to hand something up. The rest of the time I spent copying the ten-shilling note I'd got for my birthday.

A bell sounded unevenly through the blustery wind. It was dinner time. I made a dash for it, but the rain pelted down before I reached the refectory door. Between the smell of cabbage and the thought of the exams I felt sick. Mags had saved me a place. I thanked her and noticed she'd dirtied my plate with gravy to make it look as if I'd eaten.

'It was foul,' she explained. 'But you're in luck. Mother Borgia got called away and there's a treat for pud.'

A Sister came up and placed a bunch of spoons on the table.

Mags examined the clover in my buttonhole and said, 'Look, Sister. Marian's found a four-leafed clover.'

The refectory Sister smirked. 'There's three kinds of luck you know, girls. Good luck, bad luck, and no luck at all.'

'Miserable old bag, don't mind her,' Mags said after she'd gone. 'Wish for honours in the exams.'

'Honours? It'd be a miracle if I got a pass.'

She stared in disbelief.

'Honest to God, Mags, I haven't a clue.'

'How can you talk of failing, Marian, you're the oldest in the class?' Dunla said, looking up from her book.

'No, I'm not,' I lied. But it was true, I'd been kept back a year in my old school in the hope that I'd catch up.

'What year were you born, then?' she asked.

I hesitated and blushed, trying to work it out. Just then a cheer went up as large bowls of trifle were carried in by the Sisters. There was a rush to serve and bowls came swiftly down the table as hands shot up for seconds. The sight of everyone wolfing it down put me off.

The trifle looked pretty covered in mock cream and silver balls. My eye was caught and held as one of the balls moved. It was followed by a leg waving feebly through the cream. I picked it out and an ant engorged with trifle lay squirming in my hand. More followed. I lined them up on the side of my plate wondering whether to tell the others. Nudging Mags I showed her the ants.

'Holy shit, water quick,' she said and grabbing a jug went off to get some.

Dunla, halfway through her second helping, asked what was wrong.

'There's ants in the trifle. It's alive with them.' I showed her my plate. She watched wide-eyed as they struggled to get free. 'D'you know it's impossible to kill them,' I told her. 'Stamp on one and it'll walk away, grind it beneath your feet and it'll still carry on. They're said to be cleverer than humans and would take over the entire planet if it wasn't for their size.' Dunla's hand went to her mouth, but I couldn't stop.

'They'll probably thrive in your stomach, the conditions are perfect. Warm and moist with food coming in for them to gorge on. Of course they'll lay eggs, and when it gets too crowded they'll emerge at whatever exit takes their fancy. It could be the ear, nose or mouth. They may even burrow their way through the skin.'

I knew I'd gone too far. Dunla's chair fell back in her hurry to get up, but it was too late. Cupping her hands over her mouth she vomited. Some of it spurted from between her fingers and sprayed all over the table.

The word went around fast. Everyone began dissecting their trifles. The juniors started to whinge and called for Sister.

'I'm glad I didn't eat mine,' I said and flicked an ant off my plate. Nobody was listening. The refectory was in an uproar. After what happened to Dunla, everyone headed for the door. At that moment Mother Borgia appeared and got stuck in the crush.

'Would everyone please return to their place immediately,' she ordered grimly.

No one took any notice. Mother Borgia caught hold of a junior and shook her. The girl in tears pointed to me.

Mother Borgia let her go and pushed her way forward. 'What is the meaning of this, Marian O'Dea?'

'I don't know why you're picking on me,' I protested. 'There's ants in the trifle, Mother Borgia. Live ants. Everyone's eaten them. It's made Dunla really ill, she might even be poisoned. It's the Irish exam tomorrow. Dunla would never live it down if she failed that.'

'I'll deal with you later,' said Mother Borgia sternly and went off to attend to her pet.

Luckily she couldn't find any reason to blame the commotion on me. The Sisters had left the trifle out on the windowsills to set and an army of ants had marched in. Peaches and cream were served at supper that evening to save face. For once the cream was real, the same as the nuns and priests always got. Nobody felt much like eating, so I had three helpings. It was a pity to let it go to waste.

That night everyone smuggled their Irish books up to the dorm. I tried studying under the blankets, memorising 'A Day at the Sea' in Irish. It'd do for most essays we were likely to get like: 'A Day Out', 'My Birthday', 'A Favourite Treat', or 'The Holidays'.

You'd only have to change the first sentence. After learning off a few lines my eyes kept closing. Instead I got out the book Mags had lent me. She said it was probably banned and to keep it under the mattress.

The book had diagrams of men and women with the names of their different parts and explained about female egg cells and the male seed or sperm. I remembered the time Celine missed her periods. The doctor told her she could get pregnant from sitting on a boy's knee. I always wondered how the seeds could get up your leg. One of the diagrams showed that women had three openings down there, which was strange as I thought there were only two.

We weren't encouraged to look at our bodies. Not that you had much of a chance. Bath time was only fifteen minutes, and you were supposed to wear shifts and soap yourself under cover. Nobody bothered, and they all hung in the bathroom like shrouds. The nuns still wore theirs, of course.

It was definitely a sin to touch yourself down there. Especially when you woke from a dream with an amazing feeling and wanted it to go on for ever. The dreams only came now and again, but there were ways of getting the feeling back, like finding a bike with a good saddle to ride, or even staying on the bus till the last minute when it reached your stop. Once when I was small, I got a girl to stroke me there with one of the cooking apples stored in the shed.

I decided to check myself to make sure everything was normal, but even with my magnifying mirror it was difficult to see through the fuzz of fair hair. I'd shaved it off when it first appeared, but it grew back straight away. To get a better look I put my legs up and was trying to find the third opening when a sound made me freeze. Before I could do anything the bedclothes were yanked back and a powerful torch shone down. Mortified I tugged at my nightdress. To my horror Mother Borgia was standing over me. Her eyes widened in disbelief. She shone the torch all over the bed, then lunged forward and snatched up the book, torch, mirror and even my toothbrush which just happened to be lying on the pillow. Her usually chalk-white face was on fire and she turned and left the dormitory without a word.

After the ants, I thought, this was the end and wondered what in the name of God was she doing prowling around the dormitory. Why did she pick my cubicle when all the others were studying too? You could tell from the glow coming from behind all their curtains. I lay there petrified for hours waiting to be hauled out, but nothing happened and I must have drifted off.

Next morning I was forbidden to speak to anyone and made to sit at the infants' table in the refectory. After breakfast, Mother Borgia told me to go straight to the dormitory and remain there until sent for.

When I tried to say something, she held up her hand.

'Your actions speak louder than words,' she said and looked at me as if I was something she'd scraped off the back of her shoe.

When I went to the dorm I found my trunk had been brought down. Surely they weren't going to throw me out? Then Mags burst in wanting to know what was going on? She said rumours were flying round that I'd been expelled. I just told her the bit about being caught in bed with her book.

'Do they know it's mine?' she asked looking scared.

''Course not.'

'Thanks for not telling.' Her face relaxed into a smile and she squeezed my arm.

I didn't want any sympathy and began clearing out my locker, thinking it was like the first time we'd met, only then I'd been full of hope.

'Have you been expelled?' she asked.

'I don't know.'

'Well, don't do anything till you're sure. It might be just a scare.'

I told her to go, afraid we'd be caught. We swore we'd write and always keep in touch, but I knew she was off to Spain after the exams to work as an au pair.

My parents were waiting nervously in the parlour.

They'd arrived in Mellon's taxi thinking it was an emergency. It was a shock to see them with Mother Borgia and my torch, mirror, Mags's book and, of course, the toothbrush laid out on the table in front of them.

'I have spared your parents some of the details of what happened last night,' Mother Borgia began.

As she spoke my mother looked mortified and my father studied the wall as if he'd nothing to do with any of us. Mother Borgia went on to say I still had a chance to redeem myself if I told them who gave me the book. They waited in silence.

'Go on, tell the nun,' my mother urged.

But I couldn't even if I hadn't promised Mags.

Then Mother Borgia started on about the pain I had caused my parents, and how she couldn't allow corruption of this sort to continue, leading others astray.

As she spoke I concentrated on her mouth which stayed in a straight line, but drooped at the sides when she stopped. 'I'll give you one last chance, Marian,' she said finally. 'Where did you get this book.'

In the silence that followed my mother kept making faces trying to get me to tell her what she wanted. Then her eyes went up to heaven as Mother Borgia began again. 'Very well then, you leave me no choice.' She turned to my parents. 'As you can see, Mr and Mrs O'Dea, I have done my best, and now I must ask you to remove Marian from this school.'

My mother looked appalled, and I don't know about my father, because I walked out unable to stand another minute of it.

As we were leaving, Mother Superior, whom we rarely saw, came out to the door and gave me a copy of the *Imitation of Christ*. She said she hoped it would help me in my journey through life.

Miriam Dunne

My mother sat tight-lipped in the car. She couldn't say anything in front of Mellon. My father stared out the window the whole way home without meeting my eye.

Chapter 13

My father had changed. I noticed it after I'd been home a few weeks. The fight had gone out of him. He'd always moaned about money but this time it was different. There was no talk any more about us ending in the poorhouse, or did we think it grew on trees. When I asked him for money he just shook his head, and from the look in his eyes I knew it was useless to press him. He slept a lot, dozing off in front of the fire, the newspapers in a heap around him. On Sundays he stayed in bed altogether. My mother said it was a bad sign but she wouldn't say of what.

He promised to look out for another school for me, a cheap day school this time, but nothing ever came of it. I mooned around the house wondering what to do. I couldn't even go out much as my clothes had begun to look childish. I brought them around to the dressmaker hoping she'd restyle them, but she threw up her hands and said she hadn't the time.

My father was worried I'd become a financial burden like Celine and urged me to do something that would bring in some money. I decided to do a secretarial course although I never wanted to work in an office. A Miss Boyle who lived up the road gave classes in shorthand and typing or, as my mother called it, business studies.

Miss Boyle was an invalid and gave her classes from a wheelchair. I never saw any of her other pupils. The classes were deadly, but Miss Boyle was all right. The typing course consisted of her putting on a record and listening attentively to see that I typed in time to the music. She allowed me to copy shorthand straight from the book, to get the feel and flow of it, she said. I became very fluent, but could never read anything back.

Celine only worked now and again, the rest of the time she sat round impeccably groomed waiting to be discovered. She'd barely spoken to me since I got back except to ask once what my plans were. Before I could reply she started talking about herself. She was out a lot, being seen at the right places. One day she got her periods in town and arrived home in a taxi. My mother thought it extravagant but didn't say anything. The only time she'd ever taken a taxi was when she had all her teeth out. She couldn't speak with all the blood, but you could see the pain in her eyes. She wrote a note to us saying she was sick of the dentist prodding around in her mouth and had them all out to be done with it.

Celine's pains miraculously disappeared when her agent rang and offered her work as an extra with one line in a film. It turned into a large speaking part in a major new film when my mother told Gertie over the hedge next morning.

When Celine started work my mother waited on her hand and foot. She was let stay out till all hours and didn't have to hand up a penny. I was desperate to find work and get some money. The want ads were no help. The only jobs going were for hotel chambermaids. One ad caught my eye:

MODELS WANTED – FREE HAIRSTYLES.

I rang them up and made an appointment. They gave

me a style called the cat's lick. My hair was backcombed into a flick-up and sprayed heavily with lacquer. I had to hold it under a tap in the ladies' room to flatten it.

The salon was over a coffee bar called the New Amsterdam. They'd a sign in the window looking for waitresses. There was nowhere like it in Dublin. It was dark and mysterious inside with a candle on each table, and all their cups and saucers were transparent. Celine often went there with her friends, as it was full of actors and models. I wondered if I'd the nerve to apply as I could only add up on my fingers and it was so dark, with my eyesight I might mix up the orders.

Celine had a fit when she heard. 'What'll I do if my friends see you?' she screamed, and banged around the house threatening to leave home if I worked as a waitress. That'd be great, I thought, and went to phone them. They sounded really nice, but then they asked could I work till after midnight some nights. I said yes, not wanting to believe that was the end of it as there was no way of getting home after the last bus at half eleven.

Next morning Celine grudgingly announced there was work going on the film for extras.

'Could Marian go, do you think?' my mother asked timidly.

'I suppose so.' Celine shrugged.

My mother was so all over her with gratitude I had to leave the room in case I said something drastic.

We got up first thing next morning to go to the studio. It was pitch dark and reminded me of Christmas. I felt so excited at breakfast I laughed when my stomach kept rumbling. Celine was in a foul humour and told me if I didn't shut up I could forget it. There wasn't a sinner about as we waited for the bus. Only the moon, surrounded by thick clouds like fields of snow, shone down. To keep warm I walked up and down flapping my arms.

'Once we get to the studio you're not to come near me, is that clear?' Celine said irritably. I nodded.

'Answer properly, you bitch,' she snapped.

'But you said not to talk,' I protested.

'Stupid cow.' Her face turned really sour and I was glad when the bus came charging up the hill flooding the road with light. Celine flashed a smile at the conductor when we got on. My mother always said she was a street angel and house devil and if she stayed at home long enough the badness would take over completely. We'd the bus to ourselves. It took off at full speed, throwing us together in the seats. Celine turned to me.

'By the way, I must warn you, there's this guy at the studio who's an absolute bastard.'

'Who's that?' I asked, wondering why she sounded almost friendly.

'His name's Clair, he's only a stand-in.'

Clair was an unusual name I thought. There was a girl at school who'd a brother called Clair. She looked a bit like Brigitte Bardot and was dead clever. Her name was Eva and she was the one who had the picture of Richard Burton on her locker and pretended it was her brother.

'Why's he a bastard?' I asked.

'He tried to empty a bottle of Guinness over my head at a party.'

'He didn't!' I tried not to sound delighted that someone had at last seen through Celine. 'What did he want to do that for?' I asked, but she told me to shut up and drew her coat around her. I was sitting on the hem of it and she yanked it from under me and turned to look out, but it was so dark all she could see was her reflection pouting back in the window.

The film studios were on a large estate outside Bray. They were built like a barracks without any windows and dwarfed the big house. Celine told me in a whisper, as if we were in church, that the big house was reserved for the stars only, but she'd managed to slip in for lunch one day with the help of a well-known actor. Wow, big deal of the day, I thought and followed her through a door marked: SILENCE. DO NOT ENTER WHEN RED LIGHT IS ON.

Inside, the walls were padded and covered in chicken wire. We picked our way through a maze of scenery to a dimly lit set where someone was hammering so loudly my eyes kept closing automatically. Celine cut me with a look and went off to join a group of policemen wearing old-fashioned helmets. They all embraced and called her darling. I edged away from them into the scenery at the back to where some extras were hanging about.

'Are you an actor?' I asked someone who looked on his last legs with TB. He sucked hard on a butt and stared straight ahead.

'You won't get much outa him at this hour,' said a woman my mother would call 'common'. She was huge and spread over the bench like a deflated balloon. I asked if she was an extra.

She nodded. 'I been in all the fillums here. They wouldn't make one withou' Marcella.' She grinned, showing a mouthful of gums.

'Do you like it?' I asked.

'Like it? Sure it's an education. If I'da stuck to charrin'

I'd never have known the half of it, an' wouldn't it be a terrible thing to die guessin'?'

'What d'you have to do?'

'Nothin' much. Sittin' roun' most the time waitin'. It's money for jam.'

A man I'd never seen before came up and caught my arm excitedly.

'Darling, have I told you I discovered the most amazing way of thickening your eyelashes?'

He had orange hair brushed back like wings and wore violet eyeshadow. Beneath a black moustache his full mouth glistened. 'You take a lighted candle,' he said, throwing back his head to demonstrate, 'and carefully drip the wax in clusters on to your eyelashes. It's so easy, d'you see?' he said squeezing my arm till it hurt. 'Must go, Mickey's in a mood and he's watching.'

'Isn' tha' one a righ' lookin' eejit? Would yeh believe he's a beautiful wife an' a family of childrun. Who'd a thought he had it in him?' Marcella said as in amazement I watched him go.

'Who's Mickey?' I asked.

'He's a huge job here hirin' and firin' the extras. Though he does be very good to me. Has me ou' in every fillum, childrun an' all. Tha's him there in the glasses chattin' to Monty Seaman the director.'

She nodded, pointing out two stout men, one in cowboy boots, the other with glasses perched on his bald head. Close by, an amazing-looking boy sat reading on one of those canvas chairs reserved for the stars.

'Is he a star?' I asked Marcella.

'The one with the buke? No, he's one of us. Isn' he a smasher?' She bunched her cheeks into a smile and rolled her eyes. Old bag, I thought, imagine her thinking of him like that. I went over for a look when a voice on the megaphone called the extras on to the set.

'Tha's us. Are yous comin'?' Marcella heaved herself up and lumbered off.

The boy didn't move. He'd a mass of black curly hair and wore a trench coat lined with fur. I squinted to see what he was reading but he suddenly glanced up and caught me looking. His eyes went straight through me. I nearly died and in my hurry to get away accidentally brushed against him.

The set had a row of old-fashioned shops down one side. All the extras had gathered against a blank wall on the opposite side.

'Come here 'ill I tell yeh,' Marcella called me over and warned me to stay out of sight. If we were seen too much we wouldn't be asked back.

A man in front shushed her as Mickey came up. He winked at Marcella and, in a petulant voice, as if talking to children, told us where to walk when the action began. Then he waved to someone, a bell rang and lights flooded the set. 'Quiet, stand by for rehearsals,' a voice came over the megaphone, and a camera on wheels came slowly up the street. It stopped outside a tailor's shop where a man appeared dressed like Sherlock Holmes. He took out a watch and chain, checked the time, and looked anxiously up and down before hurrying off with the camera at his heels. They kept doing it over and over again.

'What's the point of walking up and down if the cameras aren't on us?' I asked Marcella.

'Ours not to reason why. Ours just to do or die,' a man in front said with an English accent. Each time they cut the scene, he balanced on one foot and wouldn't budge till they started again. 'It's for continuity,' he said when I asked.

At lunchtime I looked everywhere for the boy but there wasn't a sign of him. Celine was playing queeny in the canteen offering our lunch round to everyone.

'Leave some for me,' I whispered, sitting beside her.

'You can take the lot,' she said angrily and dumped it in my lap.

There were only two boiled eggs left. I ate one, but my throat went dry with Celine watching like a hawk. I put the other away but she kicked my foot and told me to get rid of it as it smelt of fart. No one took any notice when I offered it around.

'They can't hear you,' Celine smirked.

I tried again turning red. A hand went up at the back.

'I'll have it,' a voice said. It was the amazing-looking boy. He caught it easily and smiled a thank you.

'That's the bastard I was telling you about,' Celine whispered angrily.

Jesus, so he's the one who can see through her, I thought, and got up quickly and left the room in case he'd think I'd anything to do with her.

I didn't see him again that day as we were sent home early. Some of the men stayed on for a shoot-out scene with the policemen.

That night I lay awake thinking about the boy and went over my honeymoon dream. It's set in a room with a balcony overlooking the sea and there's this grating noise tropical insects make in films. I'm lying in a canopied bed all perfumed and bathed and wearing a negligée so fine it can be drawn with ease through my wedding ring. When the bathroom door opens, this guy comes out wearing silk pyjamas with piped seams. He takes me in his arms and we have a long lingering kiss before disappearing beneath the covers. He's always been faceless before, but now he's the boy I saw today. I kept going over it, stopping each time we went under the covers. I didn't know what happened next.

Next day we were given costumes to wear. Marcella said we were in luck as it meant more pay. I didn't recognise myself in a long blue suit with fitted jacket and button-up boots and stepped aside saying excuse me to a mirror thinking I was someone else.

The boy passed me on the stairs wearing a long black cloak, and gave me this piercing stare. It's only the way he looks at people, I tried to reason with my jumping heart. In the studio there was always a group around him as if they owned him or something. One day without thinking I went up and asked him had he a sister called Eva? When he nodded, I told him we'd been at school together, sounding all gushy and excited. The group around him stared. So what, their faces said. He waited for me to go on but I couldn't think of anything else to say and went off feeling a fool.

Every evening a coach left for the city centre stopping to let people off along the way. Celine wouldn't be seen dead in it and always got a lift. One night the bus emptied at Landsdowne Road except for the boy and an old guy at the back.

'Must be a match on,' I said turning to where he sat two rows behind. He didn't answer but rooted round in his pocket and produced a box of matches. I thanked him and asked how he liked it at the studio.

'OK. It's money I suppose.'

'Do you know you're the image of your sister except you're dark and she's fair.'

'Oh yeah?'

His long hands gripped the seats as he strained to see out. The windows were plastered with muck sealing us off from the world outside. In case he thought I was too keen I turned away and waited for the bus to slow down so I wouldn't have to shout.

'Are you a student?' I asked when it finally came to a stop. There was no reply. I turned but he wasn't there any more. He'd jumped off at the traffic lights without a word. All I had was his box of Friendly matches.

After that I followed him everywhere as Marcella said there was only a few days of filming left. He never caught me staring at him again. It's like the sun, if you stare at it directly you can't see it so well.

There always seemed to be someone with him or else he'd his head stuck in a book. In desperation I sat on the arm of his chair one day and asked if it was any good?

'I suppose so. I've read it often enough,' he said and barely looked up. I managed to see the title later in the tea queue. It was called *Crime and Punishment* which was disappointing as my mother read nothing but crime thrillers and somehow I thought he'd be above it.

We were so close in the queue I could touch his jumper and got this terrible urge to burrow into it when he suddenly turned round and asked if I'd lend him a shilling?

'D'you want anything else?' I asked getting excited.

'I wouldn't mind a bacon sandwich if you can afford it. I'll pay you back tomorrow.' He smiled and all the seriousness left his face.

To make sure we'd stay together I asked him to look for somewhere to sit while I got the food. He agreed and went off. A song started up in me as I counted the change and willed the queue to hurry.

'You can go now, you won't be needed again today,' a voice said. I turned. It was Mickey, the man in charge of extras. He said it again as I just stared.

'I have to get someone a cup of tea,' I protested, but he steered me firmly by the elbow out of the queue and said he'd see to it.

'But he wants something else and he's no money.'

'I've said I'll deal with it.' His voice rose. Heads turned and I had to leave for fear he'd fire me and I'd never see the boy again.

Next morning Celine couldn't get on her make-up and we arrived late at the studio in a panic. They hadn't even started. Everyone was just standing around waiting.

Marcella waddled over to me excitedly. 'There's been a hold-up. Your one's off sick – the star's stand-in. I tol' Monty Seaman yeh'd do grand.' She caught hold of my arm. 'C'mon an' meet him. Now's your chance.'

'No, Marcella.' I shrank back embarrassed. People were watching.

'There's nothin' to it. All yeh do is stand there.'

'I can't.'

'Sweet Jaysis, wha' ails yeh? It's double pay. I'd stand on me head for tha' kinda money.'

I smiled, imagining Marcella's head supporting her huge frame upside down. She took my arm and brought me over to where the director and Mickey were sitting.

'Here she is, Mister. Wouldn' she do lovely?'

They glanced up. Monty Seaman looked me up and down while Mickey stared past me as if I didn't exist. Then Seaman said something to Mickey who nodded and, without looking, told me to see the wardrobe mistress and report on set immediately.

Marcella beamed. 'What'd I tell yeh?'

I thanked her, still unsure of what I was getting into. But she was right. I'd just to stand there while they set up the lights. It was to save the stars from getting tired. You only had to be the same colouring and height and wear similar clothes.

I was standing in for Simone Bourget, a French actress. She was a peroxide blonde and wore loads of make-up. Someone said they'd managed to touch her hair once and it felt like concrete.

Mrs Short, the wardrobe mistress, fitted me out in a tight-laced bodice, frilled underskirts and high boots. Her mouth was full of pins. I was afraid to ask her anything in case she swallowed one.

The set was a bedroom with a huge four-poster bed. The floor was marked in chalk with two large crosses beside the bed. I was told to stand on one. I wondered who the other was for when a blinding battery of lights came on. Then the boy appeared with a book in his hand. He stood on the cross inches away from me. I barely came up to his neck which was just as well. If I looked him in the eye I'd have passed out.

'You're Clair, aren't you. How d'you spell that?' I asked but couldn't catch his reply as a voice barked out angrily, 'No talking on set.' It was Mickey on one side, watching in the dark. We stood like statues while they measured distances and arranged the lights. An hour passed in a flash. With Clair beside me I could have stayed there all week.

We broke for lunch. I was too excited to eat and sped off to the dressing room to do myself up. Jesus,

I thought, what a break. Now I don't need an excuse to get close to him any more.

After lunch I had to lie on the bed while Monty Seaman peered at me through some contraption. Clair sat at the side, engrossed in his book. Then Mr Seaman started fooling around pursing his lips and pretending to make a pass at me. The crew all laughed. It made me want to puke. I felt like a piece of meat. Who did he think he was, strutting around with his fat belly and cowboy boots with everyone falling over backwards trying to please him.

When they asked Clair to lie down beside me I almost stopped breathing. He had to put his arm around me. I tried to pretend we were alone but everywhere I looked there were faces watching. At first I couldn't look at Clair, but then I noticed his eyes moving from side to side. He'd held on to his book, and was reading it propped up on the pillow behind me. I wondered if he felt anything like I did, lying so close together. A little pulse in his neck was throbbing up and down. I wondered why and couldn't take my eyes off it.

When we finished for the day Mickey called me over before I had a chance to talk to Clair. He kept me waiting at one side and then told me Miss Bourget's stand-in would be back tomorrow and I wouldn't be needed again. By the time I got away Clair had left.

Chapter 14

They threw a party on the last day. A battery of lights shone down on the set. It was a miserable affair, no music or dancing. People just stood round in groups wilting after the early start and long day's work.

I sat on a flight of stairs leading to nowhere and watched people drift off in pairs. It was my last chance with Clair and there was no sign of him anywhere.

I saw Celine with her friends and ducked behind the set winding my way round through the scenery at the back. Then I spotted Clair by the door sitting on a canvas chair. Some extras were sitting on a bench nearby. In front of them an American was holding forth about the dreamlike quality of Antonioni and Bergman.

I sat at the end of the bench. Clair, with one hand propped under his chin, sat staring into space. There was a woman beside him, but they couldn't have been together as they weren't talking. She was too old for him anyway and looked as if she was growing out of the chair.

The American extra paused for a reaction but got none. The extras sat slumped on the bench nursing half-empty glasses of stout. He started off another story about Orson Welles and a busty Spanish chick. No one was listening but the minute he offered them a whiskey they sprang to life. As they stood up, the bench rose with them, and I slid off on to the floor.

'Would you like a drink?'

I looked up and nearly died. Clair was standing there. He helped me up and I sat back on the bench embarrassed. The older woman passed us smiling.

'Who's that?'

'Some American moron from Trinity.'

I had meant the woman but let it go.

'But he must have brains if he's at university.'

'What gave you that idea? They're the worst kind. He's over here on a Guggenheim, working on some crazy thesis. Probably something obscure like the phallic significance of the Gaelic round tower.' He smiled.

'Oh yeah.' I smiled back not understanding a word. So I asked him what he did, to change the subject.

'Architecture, writing. Music too. I play trombone.'

Jesus, I thought, he must be brilliant doing three things and writing music as well.

'What music do you like?' I asked.

'Modern jazz. Are you interested?'

'Hmmm.' I nodded but hadn't even heard of it.

'How about Monk?'

'Oh yeah, great.'

There was a silence, my mind went blank and I couldn't think of anything to say.

'What do you do with yourself?' he asked.

'Me? I'm a late developer.'

He looked puzzled.

'I mean my periods came late and I think it holds you back. I had them forced on in the end.'

'That sounds a bit drastic.' His eyebrows went up. They were jet black like his hair, and his eyelashes were so long they curled back on themselves. It was hard to look at him, as a fluttering had begun deep down inside me. He waited for me to go on.

'Yes all my friends got theirs ages ago and they seem to have . . .' I trailed off lamely as Monty Seaman strolled past us with his arm around a young actress. He noticed the two of us sitting together and gave us a filthy look. When they'd gone I turned to Clair.

'What's he doing with her? Isn't he married? Wasn't his wife on the set the other day? What would a girl like that see in him? Did you see his belly.'

Clair shrugged. 'I suppose she got what she wanted, now it's his turn.'

'What do you mean?' I asked.

He reached out and examined my earring. The slight touch of his finger sent the flutterings charging through me.

'Enjoying the party?' he asked.

'Not much.'

'Let's get out of here?'

'Yes, let's.' I smiled, agreeing too quickly. 'But I have to make a phone call first.'

'OK. Meet you outside when you're ready.'

My father sounded huffed when I rang and wanted to know exactly where I was, who I was with and how did I propose getting home now that the last bus had gone. I explained it was the last day of the film and a whole gang of us were going to the Top Hat to celebrate. He warned me to stay with the group at all times and not to be out too late. I agreed and rang off relieved. Clair was waiting outside in a battered two-seater.

'Mind where you stand,' he said as I climbed in. I could see what he meant. Most of the floor had rusted away.

'Where to?' he asked, pressing the starter.

'How about the Top Hat?'

'Dancing?'

I nodded, watching the road fly past beneath us as we drove away. I was terrified of falling through the floor and being run over by the back wheels.

'My parents have a weekend place near here.' He looked over and saw me clinging to the door. 'Relax, it's all right. But be careful of the door. It's fallen off a few times already.'

I was relieved when we pulled up outside the dance hall. A crowd hung round watching the cars come and go. I remembered the times I'd waited, hoping for a lift home and noticed the smaller guys always drove bigger cars. The opposite must also be true, I thought, as I watched Clair unwind his long legs from the car.

I left him at the ticket office and went to the ladies. Two girls in summer dresses and matching black cardigans stood chatting by the mirror. They paused briefly as I edged past them, and locked myself in a cubicle. 'It was bound to happen,' one of them said. 'She threw herself at him. D'you remember that time when she was in hospital and heard he was going out with someone else? She ran off down the fire escape in her nightdress and hailed a taxi to go all over town looking for him.'

'She didn't,' the other one giggled.

'She did, and now his parents have cut him off without a penny. He can't even finish his degree. They'll be out on the streets.' There was a wave of music and the door slammed. I pulled the chain and wondered had they never felt mad about anyone.

My heart sank when I saw the dance floor. It was packed tight with bodies swaying together under a canopy of smoke. I waved to Clair and we elbowed our way on to the floor. He held me lightly, at arm's length, and we began to move. The music throbbed and a voice crooned:

'Only you can make this change in me, for it's true you are my destiny . . .'

Couples smooched past, locked together, eyes closed. One girl had to hold up her partner he was so locked with the drink. Spots of light darted round the room as a crystal ball revolved slowly above our heads.

'This used to be called The Crystal,' I shouted.

'Oh.' A look of pain crossed his face as the music reached its climax.

'What's the matter?'

'The trumpet player's flat,' he winced.

As the band stopped there was a great surge towards the bar.

'Let's sit the next one out?' Clair asked. I nodded.

As we left the floor I suddenly heard my name called out.

'Did you hear that?' I nudged him.

He shook his head. 'How can you hear anything through this racket?'

'You're not enjoying it?'

'It's not exactly my scene.' He smiled.

Christ, I thought, surely he doesn't want to leave me already. We were getting pushed by the crowds towards the bar.

'Would you like to come back for a drink?' he asked.

'Yeah, OK,' I said, not smiling this time, trying to keep the flutterings under control. 'Can you wait here for a second?' I asked, and left him by the bar.

'Yes,' said the woman in the ticket office, 'somebody was looking for you but they've rung off.' She directed me to the phone box. I dialled home again and my father answered immediately.

'What's the matter?' I asked.

'It's your mother, she's worried,' he lied.

'But I told you where I was and there's a crowd of us. It's embarrassing if you ring.'

'All right, dear.' His laugh sounded forced.

'Anyway, we're off for a meal somewhere.'

'All right, I'll explain to your mother. Have a good time.'

I rang off and joined Clair at the bar.

'Everything all right?'

'Yeah, it's nothing.'

The band started again. He tossed back his drink and said, 'Let's go.'

The house stood in darkness surrounded by trees away from the road. He led the way up the path.

'There's no keys, we'll get in round the back.'

It was dark round the side. Cobwebs from the trees brushed against my face. I followed him closely, our feet silent on the soft earth.

'I've a knife somewhere.' I waited while he rooted in his pockets. A cat wailed through the night, piercing the silence.

'Can't see a thing,' I said stumbling on a rock.

'OK. I have it now.'

There was a scraping sound, and then a click as the window sprang open. His face flared up as he struck a match and lit a candle perched inside the window. 'There's no electricity. It hasn't been turned on yet.' Hoisting himself up, he disappeared inside. 'I'll give you a hand,' he said, reaching back.

'It's all right.' I tried pulling myself up, but found

I couldn't move. I told him my heels were stuck in the muck.

'Oh, I forgot, the garden's been dug. They're trying to get rid of a family of rats.'

I took off my shoes and scrambled up the ledge. He caught me as I jumped.

'This way,' he said and picked up the candle. He led the way to a room filled with books. A double bed stood against the wall beside a stone fireplace. Two music stands faced the window, sheets of music lay scattered round.

'Do you practise here?' I asked.

'No, my parents. They're both musicians.' He knelt by the fireplace. 'I'll soon get this going,' he said and set a match to the fire laid in the grate. Sparks flew out as the brushwood caught, it crackled and hissed, the room grew brighter.

'Who sleeps here?' I asked.

'My parents, they're doing up the bedroom.' He waved to an old record player. 'Put on a record if you like.'

I picked one out called 'Crepuscule with Nellie', and wound the thing up. A great moaning like banshees wailing filled the room. Jesus, I thought, imagine trying to dance to that, you'd bust a gut.

'Monk,' he explained.

'I know. What's this?' I picked up a jazz poster from the pile on the table.

'Just some posters I did. We're doing a concert next week.' He opened a cupboard in the wall and took out a bottle. 'There's only whiskey,' he said, holding it to the light.

'Did you draw it yourself?'

'Yeah.' He poured the drinks.

'Can I keep one?'

'Sure.' He handed me a glass. 'The tap's in the garden. Can you drink it neat, or will I get some water?'

'No, it's fine,' I said, gagging on the first sip. The music ground to a halt. He went over to the record player and wound the handle up fast. Selecting a record, he set the needle down gently.

' "Round Midnight",' he said and put his arms around me. The kiss put me off. It was so wet. I was sure half my make-up came off. His hand moved upwards and caressed my padded bra. I'd sneaked it out of Celine's drawer. Someone brought it back for her from America. It was made of soft sponge and much better than the ones over here. It felt real except for the hoops. I drew back a bit, hoping he wouldn't feel them, but he let me go, and picking up his glass finished off the whiskey.

'Like another?'

'No thanks.'

'Better drive you home then, it's getting late.'

'It is.' I put my glass down. Christ, he thinks I'm just a kid and not interested. I went over to the fire and knelt down. 'It's a pity to leave this,' I said, and warmed my hands. He came over and, sitting back on his hunkers, took up the poker.

'I'll settle it down first.' Cascades of sparks flew up the chimney as he poked the fire.

'Do you spend much time here?'

'As often as I can. When my parents are in one house, I stay in the other. I like having a place to myself.'

'You're lucky, I haven't even got a room.'

'That must be awful, what do you do when you want to be alone?'

'There's a tree I have, but I'm getting too old for it now.'

112

He nodded. 'I had one too. What kind is yours?'

'A beech.'

'Mine was a hawthorn. I built a house there, used to spend hours in it.' He sat on the floor and stared into the fire, so I started asking questions to keep him there. He told me his father was a Protestant who became a Catholic to marry his mother. But he didn't believe in any of it. God, Heaven, Hell or an afterlife.

'Suppose you're wrong? Aren't you afraid of going to Hell?' I asked horrified.

'How can I be afraid if it doesn't exist?' He smiled. 'Most people believe out of fear. Being good or bad is up to you because it's what you want, not because there's someone up there telling you what to do.'

'Do you think there's someone up there?'

He smiled. 'You have to make up your own mind on that. That's why you're here.'

'Don't you believe in anything?' I asked, thinking he must've had a watered-down version of Catholicism coming from a mixed marriage.

'Sure.' He nodded.

'What?'

'Us.'

For a moment I thought he meant the two of us and my heart leapt.

'Us,' he went on, 'the human race. And in what we're doing.'

'What do you do?' I asked hoping he'd include me in his plans.

'Too many things, and life's so short, you only get one shot at it.'

'What's the point if that's all there is?' I asked.

'That is the point, that's all there is. The only thing that lives on is what you do with your life.'

He gazed into the fire as if he could see into his future. He seemed happy. I'd never met anyone like him before and, without thinking, reached out and touched the back of his neck. He turned, our eyes met and held for a long time.

'Let's get into bed,' he said gently, and standing up unbuttoned his coat. Immediately all the warning bells went off in my head. Surely to God he means on the bed and not in the bed? I thought, and watched as he took off his clothes.

'Are you all Irish?' I asked.

'What?' He paused before pulling his tee shirt over his head. He looked down at his body and laughed. 'I hope so, why?'

'Nothing, only someone said they thought you were a foreigner.'

Removing the last of his clothes, he got into bed shivering. 'It'll get warmer,' he said and, pulling up the covers, lay back. Half hidden behind a chair I started to undress. I couldn't take off my bra, he'd probably die laughing if he saw the size of my breasts. Thank God I'd worn my new slip. It was deep blue laced with cream. I was proud of it as I'd bought it with my first pay cheque from the film.

'C'mon, it's cold.'

'I thought you said it'd get warmer.'

'It will, once there's two of us. Like Eskimos. Skin against skin.' He drew the covers up like a tent as I got in. 'You're cheating,' he said and, easing off my slip, began fiddling with my bra.

'I'll do it,' I said and, unhooking it quickly, threw it across the room.

We snuggled down together. The smell from his skin reminded me of the sea. It was so different from the dry

acrid smell of my father's room. His body felt long and
slender like one of those modern sculptures. I wondered
had he ever posed for anything like that and asked him
had he done any modelling? He covered my mouth with
his and his hand encircling my stomach rose upwards
towards my breasts. They stiffened at this touch and
I waited for the laughter but there was none. I could
feel his hardness pressing against me and on impulse
reached down and touched it. God, Owen's was never
like that, but then, he's younger. And imagine the way
it springs out when they take off their clothes. I grasped
hold of it firmly, in case he thought I'd no experience.
But he shot back, curled up and groaned, 'Christ.'

'What's the matter?'

His breath was short. 'Didn't anyone ever teach you
how to hold it?' he asked.

Teach me? Sure who'd teach me, I thought. Imagine
going up to Mother Borgia and asking Please Mother,
how would you go about holding one? 'I'm sorry,' I
said, feeling awful.

'It's all right.' He began to uncurl. 'Only don't ever
squeeze it there.' He guided my hand.

I held it gently. It was smaller now. Then it began to
grow and I clasped it between my legs and held it there.
His body moved over mine and I stroked his back as he
rose and fell. His skin next to mine felt right.

But it's wrong a voice said. It's a mortal sin, and if
you die on the way home you'll go straight to Hell, you
must get up now. But I ignored the voice. It felt so good
I didn't want to get up.

The movements grew stronger and his breathing
changed. He was leaving me behind. Shudders ran
through him, he seemed in agony, but it was not the
agony of pain. Then he fell against me and gasped. I

touched him lightly, his back quivered, so I lay still afraid to move until he grew quiet. Suddenly I felt a trickle, it was wet between my legs, everything was wet. I pushed him roughly. 'Get up.'

'Whaat?'

'Get up quick and wait outside.'

He opened his eyes in disbelief. 'What's the matter?'

'I'll tell you later. Could you get some water?' He stumbled up and, dragging a cover from the bed, left the room.

God Almighty! I've destroyed his parents' bed. What a time to get my periods. Throwing back the covers, I examined the bedclothes but could see nothing.

Clair knocked on the door. 'Are you OK?'

'No, wait a second.'

I picked up the candle and ran the flame over the sheets. Nothing, not a mark, only a damp patch in the middle. I looked at my legs, body, nothing. He knocked again. 'It's freezing out here.'

Putting on my slip I sat down by the fire. 'All right, you can come in now.'

'What happened?' he asked, coming in with a glass of water.

'There's wet stuff over everything. I thought I'd got my periods.'

'You dope. That's the stuff.' He knelt down beside me.

'What stuff?'

'The stuff that makes the world go round.'

'What d'you mean? I thought it was like a seed. You know, round things like pellets.'

He smiled. I turned away and gazed into the fire. It had settled down to a quiet glow. He reached out and drew me under his cover and we lay back together. The kiss seemed right this time, and although his body felt as strong as steel against mine, he touched me gently.

Chapter 15

We met once a week after that. But the mortal sins were piling up. I knew the brown scapular could save me, with its guarantee to the wearer of a reprieve from the everlasting flames of hell if you died in a state of mortal sin. But I couldn't wear it all the time. It would have looked ridiculous in bed with Clair, two strips of brown woollen cloth hanging between my breasts and back, and joined together across the shoulders. None of it mattered so much when I was with him. It was only when I got home that I felt guilty as hell.

Whenever I thought of Clair something stirred inside me. It started with a flutter, then worked its way up, thrashing about like a bird trying to fly. It was agony the more I thought of him and I longed to be with him. I knew that if we met at that moment and did it, I'd probably die of bliss. But we couldn't. Clair was so busy studying he only went out once a week. I admired him for it and wished I could feel as strongly about something.

The last time we met he forgot to make another date. Maybe he was losing interest – all his talk was about going away. But we'd had such a nice day together. He'd hired a boat and we'd rowed out to Dalkey Island. We'd the place to ourselves, the slipway was empty. Only the gulls swooped down shrieking angrily at the disturbance. As we climbed up the island Clair pointed out my school. It seemed to have shrunk. I could barely make it out where it lay crouched amongst the rocks. Clair said he'd often been there to visit his sister, it's a wonder we never met. Just as well, I thought, with me looking such a hick in my school uniform. I turned away from the mainland and faced the sea.

The island felt so quiet, with just the gulls and the hum of the bees. Beneath us the sea stretched for miles, shimmering in the sunlight until it reached the horizon and became one with the sky. We were breathless when we reached the top. The day had turned warm and the sun was struggling through.

We flung ourselves down in the heather and began to kiss. It felt amazing doing it out of doors, just the two of us on that bit of land surrounded by the pounding sea. I stiffened when I heard a plane overhead and asked him to stop in case we were seen.

'Sure no one could see us from that distance,' he said.

'Suppose they've binoculars?' I asked.

He smiled but held still all the same. I felt him inside me, throbbing gently like the beat of his heart. I wanted to stay like that for ever. When the plane had gone I whispered in his ear not to move for a bit. We lay still. I thought about those exercises I'd read in a book somewhere. They were supposed to do wonders for your sex life. I'd practised them for ages and wondered if I'd got them right. They were meant for pregnant mothers, but I thought there was no harm in giving them a try. Clenching myself down there, I counted to ten and relaxed slowly. I did it again. Clair drew back suddenly.

'Ah shit, I've come too soon,' he gasped.

'Doesn't matter.' I cuddled up to him, pleased that it'd worked. Though I hated when he had to draw back like that. I longed for him to leave it there. But we couldn't, he'd explained. We could only do it properly during the safe period. Clair propped himself up and pointed out to sea.

'There's the mailboat. I'll be off on it soon.'

'Where are you going?' My heart leaped.

'London.'

'What for?'

'I've gone as far as I can here. I have to try the real world.'

What does he mean gone as far as he can go, I thought. Does that include me?

'How do you mean?' I asked.

'You never know how good you are here, or how bad. All they ever do here is drink themselves stupid and talk about what they're going to do. If anybody actually did get up and do something they'd tear him to pieces.'

Christ, he can't go now, I thought, we've only just met. 'I couldn't bear to leave Ireland,' I said lamely, but he didn't seem to hear. 'You're off for good then?' I added.

'I don't know. Maybe.'

'When?'

He didn't reply but picked a piece of grass and chewed it thoughtfully. He seemed miles away. I took hold of the grass and threw it aside. He looked surprised for a moment, then he bent down and kissed me. I clung to him. We rolled back together again in the grass.

A wind had got up when we returned to the pier. Clair was worried about the boat, though I wouldn't have minded being stranded there with him. The sea felt like ice but we had a quick dip and ate our picnic on the rocks chattering with the cold.

As we rowed away rats appeared from everywhere. They darted about picking up the bits we'd left for the birds. I shivered. Clair gave me his jumper. He said he wouldn't be needing it with all the rowing. I snuggled into it, breathing in his smell. The island grew smaller as we headed for the mainland. I felt sad leaving it. It'd been ours for a while and I'd had him to myself.

That night I took his jumper to bed with me and dreamt I was floating in the sea. It was filled with wisps of straw. There was nothing to hold on to. Clair came along in a boat packed to the hilt with provisions, enough to last a lifetime. I called out to him again and again, but no sound came. He went by, staring straight ahead, and rowed off into the horizon.

Chapter 16

A week went by and Clair never called. I waited in every day willing him to ring, but the phone remained silent. I kept lifting the receiver to see if it still worked, but it purred back coldly. In desperation I dialled his number and let it ring a few times hoping he'd get the message, but nothing happened. I thought of contacting him about his jumper, but if he just took it back and that was the end of it I'd be left with nothing.

I couldn't believe he was going away for good. Maybe it was an excuse not to see me any more. If only I had some decent clothes it'd make all the difference. I'd worn my pale blue every time now. It looked ridiculous on the island, all creased like a concertina and the grass stains would never come out. I had to get a job, and asked Miss Boyle what the chances were for office work. Slim she said. The competition was fierce. There were hundreds after the one job. Everyone was highly qualified or had lots of experience. There wasn't a hope unless I'd a diploma. This was really depressing. I didn't even want to be an office worker. For years I'd watched them from the top deck of the bus, grey creatures hunched over their desks, shuffling bits of paper round from nine till six. It was worse than school with no long holidays to look forward to.

'Why worry?' Miss Boyle said. 'When any day now a

nice young man will come along and whisk you off your feet and you'll settle down.' Her face creased into smiles when she said this which really annoyed me. I told her I'd no intention of settling down in a suburban house forever like my mother. In that case, she said, you'd better put your name down for the City and Guilds. She knew someone who ran a secretarial college and there'd be no problem getting me on the exam list.

The college was on the second floor over a travel bureau in Grafton Street. A hefty woman in tweeds met me on the stairs. Waving a vase of foul-smelling water she directed me to the exam room and disappeared through a door marked MNÁ.

The room was full of girls chatting happily as if looking forward to what lay ahead. Most of them wore suits, some even had hats. My mother would have approved. I hurried to the back conscious of my shoe. One of the straps had broken that morning and was held together with string.

It reminded me of school. Long rows of desks facing a teacher's throne. Each desk, slightly parted from the next, was crowned with a pale green typewriter. They looked brand new compared to the rest of the place. On the blackboard someone had written:

SHORTHAND IS A USEFUL TOOL. IT OPENS DOORS TO
MANY PROFITABLE & INTERESTING LINES OF WORK

The hefty woman came into the room clutching papers to her chest. Breathing heavily she mounted the throne and dropped them on the desk. Her chest stuck out like a shelf. She introduced herself as Miss Heaps and hoped we'd come well equipped with paper and pens. Taking out a stopwatch she eyed us and said: 'Whatever you do, don't stop. If you miss a word continue writing, with any luck it might come back to you later. To warm up, we'll start with some words, followed by brief forms. Are there any questions?'

Nobody spoke. Everyone sat with pens poised.

'I would advise you to remove pen tops and any wristwatches or jewellery you may be wearing. The extra weight will slow you down. Are you ready?' She clicked her watch and began dictating at an alarming rate. 'Band, baked, bared, board, bombed, boat, bond, both, bone, bore, bold . . .' My pen dug into the page as I tried to get them down, but every outline looked the same. There was a flurry of pages turning as Miss Heaps began the letter.

'Dear Madam, In a recent survey five hundred business-men were asked to say what qualities they especially valued in their secretary. Ten points emerged which might surprise you . . .'

The words wouldn't stay in my head long enough to be written down. I got the beginning and end, 'Should you require any further information please do not hesi-tate to contact us. Assuring you of our best attention at all times, Yours faithfully,' but there was a great gap in the middle.

'Three minutes to transcribe,' Miss Heaps called and clicked her watch.

I began with the letter while it was still fresh in my head. 'Dear Madam,' I wrote, but it didn't look right. I tried it in rough, Madam? Modom? Madame? Mesdame? They all looked queer. I thought I'd chance Madam. But then I noticed it spelt the same backwards and forwards. That couldn't be right I thought and added an e hoping for the best.

'Time's up. Pens down. Pass along your work.' Miss

Heaps's voice rose as she hurried down the aisle. I couldn't hand mine up. It was too depressing and reminded me of the History exam at school.

'You may practise on your typewriters before we start,' Miss Heaps announced as she walked around the room distributing papers. I slotted a page into the typewriter and typed Clair's name at high speed, running it all together across the page.

Miss Heaps's hand went up. 'We'll start now.' She waited while everyone inserted fresh sheets of paper. 'You have six minutes to complete the piece starting now,' she said and clicked her watch.

All the typewriters began at once. I went slowly, guiding my fingers carefully. One mistake and I'd had it as I'd only make more. A carriage shot across, followed by another, then a whole burst of them. They were all ahead of me. By the end of the first paragraph I began to breathe. Only three to go, I might just make it.

Halfway through, I still hadn't made a mistake and began to feel relieved. But then I felt something else deep inside me and thought of Clair. I crossed my legs but it grew stronger. In an effort to ease it away I pressed myself into the chair, but it flared up with such force I had to stop typing. The thought that time was running out only made it worse, so much so, I had to leave the room. The toilets smelt of Jeyes Fluid. When I turned the light on, it pinged with a flash and then went out. I locked the toilet door, but knew the feeling had gone before I touched myself there. From the café next door a voice sang plaintively:

'For all we know we may never meet again, Love me tonight, tomorrow may never come.'

I sat listening. The walls were painted two shades of green, a brown line running through the middle dividing the two. Someone had scratched a Sisters of Mercy number on the door. It's no use, I thought, I'd have to ring Clair; even just to see him for a minute would help.

The exam was over. Girls came pouring out jostling each other down the stairs.

'How'd you get on?' they shouted to each other.

'It was dead easy. I was all geared up for more complicated stuff. The typing was a cinch.'

'Are you coming for an espresso?'

'Yep. Where?'

'Next door, OK?'

They stood back as someone came up the stairs. It was my father. His face looked drained under his Sunday hat. When he saw me he smiled.

'Hello, love, how did it go?'

They watched curiously, moving aside.

'What's the matter?' I asked, embarrassed by their stares.

'Nothing.'

'Why did you come?'

He looked hurt. 'Do I need an excuse to see my girl?'

'I just wondered.' We both waited for the other to speak.

'How did you get on?'

'OK.'

'Where are you off to?' he asked.

'I'm having coffee with the girls, to compare notes, you know.'

His face fell. 'I was hoping for a stroll through the Green. It's a lovely evening.'

'I can't, not now.'

We walked down to the street together.

'Do you need any money?' he asked.

127

'No, I'm fine.'

'Here.' He pressed a ten-shilling note into my hand. 'You deserve it after all the hard work.'

I hugged him and said goodbye. When I turned to wave he was standing on the pavement. He saluted with his newspaper waiting for me to be the first to turn away.

The coffee house was packed. A juke box blared. The man behind the counter directed me to the phone. I dialled Clair's number and waited, my insides slowly dropping out. He answered on the fourth ring.

'Yes?'

'It's me. Are you busy?'

'No.'

'Aren't you working?'

'I am, but it doesn't matter.'

'I had to ring. I've just been doing this terrible exam. I got an amazing feeling in the middle of it and thought of you. It was so bad I had to leave. I hope I'm not disturbing you?' I said when he didn't answer.

'It's OK. I needed a break.'

'I wish we could see more of each other.'

'Why don't we?'

'When?'

'Come round now.'

'Now? I dunno, it's late. I'm expected home.' I waited but he didn't say anything. 'Will you be in?' I asked.

'Yes.'

'OK. I'll see how it goes.' Of course I went to see him. I practically ran all the way.

We'd a perfect night. His parents were away and we'd the house to ourselves. I'd just finished my periods so we were able to do it properly over and over again. It was frantic at first, but then we calmed down and grew

more relaxed, almost falling asleep the last time around.
After that it was impossible to get up and trudge home
through the night. It got so late in the end Clair phoned
for a taxi. While we waited he said my voice had gone
all deep from sex and I'd better watch out or everyone'd
know. I believed him at first till I saw his face.

The taxi dropped me at the end of our road. It was
pitch dark when he drove away, not a light in sight.
I crept in our gate. Luckily they'd left the back door
unlocked. Just as I went over to the switch, the light
snapped on. My father stood there. I wondered had he
been waiting all the time or had he just come down?

'That was a nice long coffee you had with the girls.'
He sounded pleasant but I knew he was raging. He
checked his watch. 'Nine hours to be exact. What have
you been doing all this time?'

'Having a bit of fun after doing exams all day, since
you won't give me enough money and I have to get a
job,' I snapped, feeling guilty as hell. This was unfair
and he looked hurt, so I made up a story about going
to a girl's house and her brother was there with some
of his friends and we played records and danced.

'Until two in the morning? What sort of parents
would put up with that kind of racket late at night?'
he wanted to know.

I didn't answer so he started asking a million questions like who was this girl? Where did she live? Didn't
she have a phone? How old was her brother? He went
on, working himself up till I turned on him. Why didn't
he ring her himself and find out. Why not wake the
whole household while he's about it, making me out
a liar in front of the lot of them.

I turned to the sink for a drink. He came up behind
me.

'What's the matter, Marian, your voice . . .'

'What d'you mean?' I asked remembering what Clair had said about my voice getting deeper after sex.

'You sound hysterical and there's no need for that. I get worried when it's so late and you're not home.' He put his arms round me. 'Let's make up and go to bed.'

Relieved I said good night, but as I left he called me back. 'Remember, Marian, if any man ever lays a hand on you I'll kill him, I swear to God.' I knew he wasn't kidding. He meant every word of it.

We met earlier after that. He was working on a short story for some competition in London. I typed it up for him, but didn't understand a word of it. We still had plenty of time to go to bed afterwards. My parents seemed to think I couldn't be up to much if I was home before ten.

Chapter 17

Easter was coming. On Good Friday I found my mother hunched over the breakfast table examining her cup from every angle. I could see she was in a mood before she spoke. She'd been up half the night trying to finish her Easter hat. She'd woken me at intervals with her muttering and cursing.

'I don't like the look of it,' she said shaking her head.

'Did you finish the hat?' I asked, helping myself to the pyramid of toast that lay in front of her.

'No, I ended up ripping the whole damn thing to pieces. Here, what do you make of it?' She handed me her cup.

'A cluster of tea leaves,' I said, taking a look.

'Oh for God's sake, Marian, there's more to it than that. That cluster means something. It's a warning. What could it be? Clouds gathering but they said the weather would hold for the weekend.'

I thought with pleasure of the days ahead. A marquee dance at the tennis club, and tomorrow, oh joy of joys, a picnic with Clair up the mountains.

'Don't be deceived, that's freak weather for this time of year. It could change at any moment. My mother always said, cast not a clout till May is out, and she was never wrong.'

With a sigh she swirled her tea round and emptied the dregs into the slop bowl. 'Have you seen what Gertie's lined up on her kitchen cabinet?' my mother asked, helping herself to toast.

'No?'

'Fetch my teeth for me and I'll tell you.'

God, I thought, you'd think she'd put them in before she came down. My parents seemed hopelessly old to me sometimes. I hated fetching my mother's teeth and waiting while she fitted them, the water they lay steeping in overnight sometimes splashing my hand. I brought them down and held the mug out without looking.

'She's a set of Coronation tins on top of her kitchen cabinet.'

'What?' I asked.

She gesticulated angrily with her teeth in her hand. 'Gertie has a new set of canisters with a picture of the Royal family smiling from every tin.'

I nodded to her teeth. She sucked them up into her gums.

'It's enough to make your blood boil. Every time I set foot in my own kitchen I'll have that bunch looking down on me. Of course she does it on purpose to annoy me. I wonder what her Easter rig-out's like? If it's anything like last year's, mutton dressed up as lamb.' She bit into her toast. 'I hope you're making your Easter dues and won't be showing me up in front of the neighbours.'

'Probably.'

'What do you mean, probably? You're going to confession I hope?'

'Yeah, but I might be out late and miss Communion Mass.'

'You'd better not if you know what's good for you.'

I let it go. Impossible to explain it'd be a waste of time going to confession if I was in a state of mortal sin before morning. But then he might not turn up. He'd lots of work to do. And supposing he wants to go off drinking with his intellectual friends. We bumped into them last week, half the time I hadn't a clue what they were talking about, and the look they gave me when I wanted to leave. And that brazen one from Trinity, the way she sat on the toilet showing all she'd got. The fat thighs on her and those silk salmon knickers around her knees, a desperate colour against her skin, but she didn't seem to notice. Imagine her talking about sex like that. Saying it was the only thing that kept her from getting constipated, that and the Guinness. Came out with it just like that, and I'm not even able to talk about it, and only feel easy doing it with my eyes shut and the lights off. They're a different breed, that university crowd. What's the point sitting in a pub half the night afraid to open your mouth and getting hazy with drink. It's a pity he doesn't like dancing . . .

'Your father never came home last night,' my mother broke in.

'What? He's never done that before,' I asked alarmed.

'Well, he did last night. Your Daddy's not all he makes out to be. D'you know he used to go off to London with that brother of his when you and Celine were little and leave me alone here to cope and I not knowing a thing about it till he walked through that door there.'

'Has he phoned?'

'Oh, with some rubbishy excuse about a pain in his stomach. Said he hadn't time for a proper lunch and ate out at some cheap place. Steak and kidney pie. From a tin, no doubt. Pure poison.'

'Did you hear from him this morning?' I asked, but she went on.

'It beats me what that brother of his was doing that he couldn't look after the shop for a minute . . .'

I left her moaning and went out to the hall to phone him. My mother followed me out wide-eyed.

'Sssssshhhh, Marian, listen.' We heard Celine banging about upstairs. 'Oh my God, I forgot. She'll be down in a minute and I haven't a penny. Quick, ring your father and ask what he proposes to do about the money situation for the weekend.'

'I'm ringing now but there's no answer.'

'Holy God, don't say he's off gallivanting with that brother of his.'

We heard Celine on the stairs and watched in silence as she descended in a pair of stilettos. The minute she saw my mother she started.

'Why didn't you wake me? You knew I had an appointment with Berry for twelve.'

'Have some breakfast, dear, you'll feel better . . .'

'Are you mad, don't you know I'm late? Give me some money.' She dragged on her coat and checked her face in the hall mirror.

'I haven't any, your father never came home . . .'

'What?' She spun round. 'But my hair's in a mess. I have to get it done.'

'Of course you do, dear, just go right ahead. Berry will get her money, I'll see to it.'

'You'd better,' Celine said viciously and went out slamming the door.

My mother let out a sigh which I ignored. I went upstairs. Celine had left the usual mess in the bathroom.

Topless bottles, scattered powder, dirty cotton wool, towels and underwear in a heap on the floor. I was tidying up knowing the effect it'd have on my mother, when I heard her call.

'Marian, there's Mellon's taxi.'

I went down quickly and joined her. We peered through the curtains as a shiny black limousine moved slowly up the road. It glinted sharply in the bright sunshine and came to a stop under the cherry tree in full bloom by our gate. 'There's your Daddy in the back, and would you look at the cut of him. He can't even get out of the car. It's just like him. If he gets a pain in his big toe he has to smother it in drink. A grown man like him, will he never grow up, and in broad daylight too. Gertie will see everything. Mother of God, would he not get out of the car. What's Mellon doing, why doesn't he help him?'

As she spoke Mellon got out of the car and came in the gate. 'Where's he been drinking this hour of the morning? Down the Quays no doubt like his mother before him,' my mother said, taking off her apron. 'That family were all the same, weak, no guts between any of them. Of course my mother warned me, she never liked the look of him, said he wouldn't last long.' She opened the door smiling.

'Hello, Mr Mellon. Grand day isn't it. Lovely for the holiday.'

Mellon jerked his thumb at the car. 'He can't get out, Missus. He's doubled up with pain.'

'Pain?' She stepped back in alarm. 'No, don't bring him in. The last time he was laid up I had to look after him. He'd a shadow on his lung and refused to go into hospital. He wouldn't let on to anyone he was ill. Six months it went on for and my poor feet up and down those stairs . . .'

I stepped on her foot as my father's face appeared haggard through the car window.

'What's the matter, Marian?' she began, but then saw his face in the window. 'You'd better take him down to the doctor's. I don't like the look of him.'

I hung back. 'Why don't you?'

'Me? I'm not dressed for it.'

I followed Mellon out to the car and slipped into the back. It pulled away noiselessly. My father sat on the edge of the seat with his head in his hands. He looked at me unable to speak. I could see from his eyes he was racked with pain. I squeezed his hand. It was cold against mine. He shifted round restlessly in his seat. His hand slipped away. I felt helpless and stared blindly out the window. The car glided to a stop outside the doctor's house. Mellon helped me with him up the steps. He staggered between us drunk with pain. I held my finger on the bell, willing someone to open the door. An old maid appeared, her face scored with lines of permanent discontent. She let us in without a word and taking hold of my father led him away. I stood alone in the gloom of the hall listening. There wasn't a sound. The front door was bordered with panes of coloured glass. Stooping down I peered through and watched the world outside change from green to amber, then red. A dog bounded up the steps and barked hysterically. I heard a shuffling behind me and stood up unsteadily. The doctor was there with a letter in her hand.

'You'll have to take him to the hospital immediately.'

We helped him into the car, the dog yelping round our feet, and sped off towards the city. My father lay back exhausted with his eyes closed. I took his hand again, but it was limp like the rest of him.

The city appeared suspended in a haze of heat. We got caught up in traffic and crawled towards the hospital. People wandered past, relaxed by the weather, taking their ease. Mellon put on a spurt as we swerved through the hospital gates. Some attendants came out and helped my father through the door. A nurse came up with a wheelchair and settled him into it. Mellon ducked back towards the car and said he'd be off now. My father reached out and gripped my arm.

'Don't leave me, Marian.'

The nurse eased him away. 'Now we mustn't make a fuss. We're just going to make you more comfortable.'

We set off down the corridor. She nodded towards the waiting room before disappearing through the swing doors. The room was ablaze with sunlight but the air inside smelt stale. An old woman hunched up in a dressing gown sat staring into space, a forgotten cigarette slack between her fingers. A thin column of smoke rose above her undisturbed. I moved about noisily, afraid she might set fire to herself. She coughed, her head sank to her chest and ash fell into the folds of her gown. The nurse came back. She took the cigarette away from her and stubbed it out.

'You can see him now, he's asking for you.' I followed her along the corridor. 'Only for a minute,' she said and opened a door.

My father looked lost in the bed, his face grey against the pillow. 'How are you feeling?' I asked.

'I'm all right.'

I crossed to the window. 'They've given you a grand view. It's lovely outside, there's a garden with trees and the sun's shining.' I looked at him but there was no response. 'There's a marquee dance tonight,' I went on. 'They say it's going to be great but I've no money . . .'

He nodded to his clothes on the chair. 'Try my coat.'

I searched the pockets. 'Nothing, only some small change.'

He looked at me helplessly. 'They're not going to cut into me, Marian, are they?'

'No, I'm sure they won't,' I lied, not knowing what they might do to him. He saw the doubt in my eyes. Two nurses came in.

'That's enough for now.' They tugged the end of his bed, it rolled away and disappeared out the door. I gazed through the window. The tree became blurred and I couldn't swallow with the pain in my throat.

A nurse came up and smiled. 'Why don't you wait outside? It could take some time. They've taken him down to surgery.'

I went out and sat on a bench wondering why in the name of God I'd asked him for money at a time like this? Worrying him just when he's about to face the thing he dreads most? I'm as bad as the others, I thought, and dug my feet viciously into the gravel path. I got up quickly and went back into the hospital. A nurse directed me to the telephone. It rang for a long time before Clair answered.

'I thought you weren't there.'

'Hello? Oh it's you. No, I was in the garden. It's lovely outside.'

'I know. It's about tomorrow. I can't come. I'm with my father in the hospital. I think he's dying.'

'Surely not. That's a bit sudden isn't it?'

'Yes, maybe you're right, but I can't make it all the same.'

'That's a pity. I'd like to have seen you before I go.'

'Go?'

'I'm off to London.'

138

Oh God, I'd forgotten.

'Are you there?'

'You've made up your mind then?'

'Yes. I've had enough of Dublin. Thought I might as well get out as soon as I can.'

'When are you going?'

'After Easter, end of the week sometime.'

'I'll give you a ring before then.'

'Yes, do. Let me know how it goes.'

'Goodbye then.'

''Bye.' There was a click and he was gone.

God, I thought, that was awful. I never got through to him at all. He can't go away, not now. He'd always seemed so vague about it. I didn't think it would happen for ages. A nurse tapped me on the shoulder.

'Are you a relative of Mr O'Dea's?'

'Yes, his daughter. How is he?'

'Follow me please.' I hurried after her. 'Is there anyone with you?'

'No.'

'Your mother?'

'She couldn't come.'

She led me into a ward. The room seemed to be full of old men. Then I noticed a young boy propped against a mound of pillows. He followed us keenly with his eyes. My father lay unconscious in the bed attached to all sorts of machines. The nurse went across to adjust one. I picked up his hand and held it wondering if he knew I was there. I felt for his pulse, hoping he wouldn't know why. It throbbed away gently. Suddenly it began to pound rapidly, then it faltered unevenly, flickered weakly and was gone. The nurse clicked a switch and made the sign of the cross. She drew up the sheet and signalled for me to leave. On the way out we passed the boy in the bed. He sat up stiffly with a look of terror on his face. I left the ward angrily, wondering what on earth a child was doing in a place like that.

Chapter 18

My mother only broke down once. It was after we came back from the mortuary. When I handed her a cup of tea she froze and stared at my father's hat on the chair. 'Where did that come from? Take it away, out of my sight,' she moaned and, shielding her eyes, rocked to and fro.

It's a bit late for that now, I thought. Why didn't you show any feelings for him when he was alive? Celine told her to pull herself together, for God's sake, there was a funeral to be arranged.

I took his hat upstairs, but wouldn't go into the room. Although we'd just seen him in the morgue I couldn't believe he was dead, but then it wasn't really him, just his body like a shell. He was laid out on a bed of stone, his head supported by a granite pillow. They'd dressed him in a brown habit, the colour he detested most. Rosary beads spilled from between his clenched hands. A Biro mark on his finger was the only familiar thing about him. I kept my eye on it, the rest of him had gone. But where? I knew he wasn't in Heaven sitting at the right hand of God, or in Hell suffering eternal damnation. He was somewhere else and it wasn't Purgatory. None of it seemed real any more. All that was left for him now was the grave: nothing could save him from that. The coffin wouldn't last long. One spadeful of earth is enough to see all the fierce activity that goes on there. Once, when I'd buried a frog and tried to dig him up a week later there was nothing left except the bit of cloth I'd wrapped him in.

The funeral had to wait till after the holiday weekend. The good weather held. At the church, people poured out from ten o'clock Mass and mingled with the funeral crowd. They chatted together in the sunshine. It was more like a social event with everyone dressed in their Sunday best. I wanted to grab hold of someone and say, Do you realise my father's dead? He was here a few days ago, walking round like you and me and now he's gone for ever.

Some of Celine's acting friends arrived and took charge of her. I heard one of them say, 'Lovely day for it, it's a scorcher.' As if we were going on a picnic. I longed for a storm to blow up, with howling gales and lashing rain, but the sky remained a piercing blue with no cloud to break it.

I hardly knew any of my relations. The two families had been at odds for years over some forgotten row. I saw an uncle embrace one of Celine's friends and call her Celine. She moved away embarrassed. My father's partner, Uncle Ted, was taking it very badly. And no wonder, my mother said, he never knew how well off he was, now he'll have to shift for himself. He looked demented in the cemetery and kept touching the coffin. He threw himself on it when we reached the grave and refused to let them bury it. Then he turned on a weeping aunt and asked her what she was crying about? Larry O'Dea meant nothing to her. She cried out he wasn't the only one who'd someone buried in Glasnevin. I felt such a sham I couldn't cry even when they'd lowered him into the ground.

After the funeral people came up to shake hands with my mother and say they were sorry for her trouble. She kept repeating like a litany, 'It's a blessing in disguise he went the way he did. He'd never have stuck being an invalid, cooped up in bed all day or in a wheelchair. That would have killed him.'

She was anxiously counting heads as everyone trooped back to our house, worried in case she hadn't provided enough food and drink. The women went off to the kitchen to give her a hand. I left them to it and went upstairs to think about my father. I was afraid if I didn't I'd lose him completely. I went over all the times we'd had, and our last row, when I'd slammed the door in his face. Then he'd knocked, and I opened it angrily to see him standing there with this great black eye. 'Did I do that?' I'd asked in horror. He nodded gravely and I threw myself into his arms. Then I heard him laugh and knew it was a joke. He'd done it himself with black polish.

I swallowed the lump in my throat as someone knocked. It was Owen to see how I was? I said fine. Then he told me about a girl whose dog had just died. She was so upset she'd cried for days. I asked him if he'd had anything to eat. He said no, so I told him he'd better go down and get some before it's all gone. When he left, I started thinking again, but it was no use, the lump had gone.

Clair rang the next day and we arranged to meet before he went away. Celine and my mother had a fit when they heard. How could I go out so soon after the funeral. It just wasn't done. They couldn't understand why I had to see him. When I went to get ready, they followed me upstairs and said it was indecent, had I no feelings. We'd a terrible row. I ran out to the garden to get away from them and had this desperate urge to bang my head against the wall till it was reduced to a stalk, like the pictures of beheaded martyrs I'd seen in a book.

We met at his parents' place near town. They lived in a semi like ours only bigger with a garage. His parents were out and he gave me this terrific hug with his dog jumping round our feet. I was afraid he'd want us to go to bed after it and started to explain why I couldn't, but he shushed me and said of course not. I'd have liked to, as it was our last day, but I felt my father was out there somewhere, watching.

We decided to go into town. Before we left Clair insisted I sat down and ate a bowl of fruit and cream.

Their house was a mess, with stacks of music everywhere and dirty dishes all over the table. This wouldn't be allowed in our house. Even when my mother was ill she insisted on getting up and hoovering the whole house before the doctor came. It was nice sitting there with his dog and all the clutter, easy and relaxed.

We took a bus into town and walked around. It was Sunday and the church bells rang out through the empty streets. When we went for a drink Clair asked about the death. I told him all about it and how unreal it felt. Between the drink and everything I ended up crying. Clair held my hand and listened till I wore myself out.

We set off again for a walk down the Quays. The Liffey stank as the tide was low. I asked him would he miss Dublin at all?

'I'll never be so glad to get away from anywhere in my life.'

'What about your family and friends?'

He didn't answer.

We stopped to watch a heron poised on a branch poking out of the mud. Clair was off in a daze. I hated him like this. It was as if he'd gone already.

'How about close friends?' I kept on trying to get a response. We started walking again. He took these great strides with his long legs.

'I was engaged once,' he said.

'To who?' I asked breathless from trying to keep up.

'No one in particular. There were seven in the family, all girls. The mother was desperate to marry them off.'

'What did she work at?'

'A model or something.'

'What happened?'

'We were too young. It was all intense. They'd even planned the wedding. Imagine, at nineteen?'

I wouldn't mind if it was you I thought.

'It's strange,' he went on. 'But we were walking along the Quays just like this. We'd been arguing about it. I was trying to explain when she handed back the ring. You should have seen her face when I flicked it into the water. It was supposed to have been her grand gesture.' He smiled. 'D'you know what her mother said when she heard we'd broken it off?'

I shook my head.

'After all the butter that boy ate in my house.'

I smiled and felt pleased, but there was a warning there not to push too hard.

A photographer snapped us on O'Connell Bridge. I saved the ticket to have it developed later. He said he'd write and let me know how things were going. We weren't able to have a proper kiss as there were

145

people around. It was awful when the bus started and he walked away. I waited on the platform as it gathered speed, hoping he'd turn for a wave, but he never looked back.

Chapter 19

Once Clair went away I decided to make a clean breast of it with a one-day retreat followed by confession, Mass and Holy Communion at the Jesuits in Milltown Park. The Jesuits were supposed to be the intelligentsia of the priesthood and more enlightened than ordinary priests.

Gertie was going too. I heard her tell my mother over the hedge that morning.

The people making the retreat were mostly older women. Father Brian, the retreat priest, was all right. He didn't give the usual lecture about Sin and Damnation, but spoke about Redemption. He quoted a lot from a book called *Brighton Rock* and asked if anyone had read it. When no one put up their hand he strongly recommended that we should all get it. It gave a perfect example of how all of us could be redeemed no matter how badly we've sinned. And how no one is cut off from the mercy of God. I saw Gertie perking up in the front row. She'd given up the drink for Lent but hit the bottle again at Easter. My mother swore she saw her use the cat to wipe the table and then toss it out the window.

I lit a candle in the church and begged St Catherine to get Clair to contact me. I hadn't prayed to her for ages, not since I'd threatened her. I was fed up praying and talking to her for years without any results. I told her if she didn't appear to me I'd never believe in her again. That night she appeared in a dream playing the piano. She looked sad and her fingers were all bleeding. The white keys were covered in blood which poured on to her lap. As the blood rose up around her she looked at me reproachfully until she was completely submerged. I woke up in a panic and promised I'd always believe in her no matter what.

The confession queue was long, four pews deep. Whispered prayers went on all round me when I joined it. Father Brian was fast, the queue kept up a constant shuffle moving sideways on their knees towards the box. As I got nearer my throat went dry and I nearly jumped out of my skin when a large woman plumped herself down beside me. She took out her beads and began to say the rosary. Little whistling sounds escaped from her as she prayed feverishly. When it was my turn I waited in the dark until he'd finished with the penitent on the other side. Then the window slid back and he was there. I couldn't see him but could smell a mixture of perspiration and hair oil. He gave a little cough of expectancy and I began, my palms damp.

'Bless me, Father, for I have sinned, it's been six weeks since my last confession.'

'Yes, my child.'

'It's this boy, Father. I think I'm in a state of mortal sin.'

'Why do you think that?' he asked.

I hesitated, terrified he'd explode with rage.

'Go on, my child,' he said encouragingly.

'We've been to bed together,' I blurted out.

'I see. Were you in a state of undress?'

'Yes, Father.'

'Did penetration take place?'

'Yes,' I said, encouraged by his voice; he didn't seem angry at all.

'How many times has it happened?'

'I'm not sure really,' I said, lying a bit.

'How do you feel about it?'

Great, I wanted to say but couldn't.

'How old are you, my child?'

'Sixteen.'

'Do you think you are mature enough for that kind of relationship?'

'Well, sort of.'

'Are you planning to marry this person?'

'Gosh no. He's gone away to England. I don't know if I'll ever see him again.'

'I think we need to discuss this matter further,' he said shifting about in his box. 'Perhaps we can arrange some meetings. Can you come to my office after the retreat?'

'Yes, Father,' I said and thought, shite. Is he not going to absolve me after all that? But to my relief he began to mutter the Latin prayers of absolution.

He finished up by giving me a penance of only six Our Fathers, six Hail Marys and six Gloris Be's. That's brilliant I thought. Mags once got three whole decades of the rosary for just letting a boy put his hand on her leg. Admittedly, it was above the knee, but the priest went berserk and told her she must never see him again as he was hopelessly insane.

Later I knocked on his office door. He was stocky and old, in his forties perhaps, and yet he didn't miss a thing. I could tell when he shook my hand the way he took me all in. When I started saying who I was he seemed to know already. How can he tell, I wondered, was it my voice?

'This boy you were telling me about. He's gone away you say?'

'Yes, Father.'

'Have you heard from him since?'

'No, Father.'

'And what are your plans for the future?'

'I dunno really.'

'Well then, I think we should definitely arrange a series of meetings for spiritual guidance. When would be the best time for you?'

Jesus, I couldn't bear this, I thought, and began to make excuses. 'The thing is, I'm a bit all over the place at the moment since my father died . . .'

'Ah, I wondered why you were wearing black,' he said slowly looking me up and down. 'All the more reason to talk to someone and sort yourself out at this difficult time. Leave me your name and address. I'll give you a chance to think about it before contacting you. Here, take my card, you can phone me at this number day or night.'

'Thanks,' I said and wondered could anyone be that desperate.

When I got home my mother said I looked the better for it. Maybe something like that might be good for Celine too.

Chapter 20

A week later Mags rang out the blue to say she was home for her brother's wedding and could we meet. 'Thank God it's a wedding for a change and not a funeral,' she added.

I told her about my father's death. She made all the right sounds but I remembered the way she kept on at me in school for going round the grounds with him arms linked.

Before I even set eyes on her I heard her heels click up the garden path and a voice through the letter box shout, 'Don't say I didn't keep in touch.' She came in like a blast of life and gave me a hug. 'Well, you haven't changed. You still look about fourteen.'

She reminded me of a Spanish gypsy with her black hair, dark skin and kiss curls planted either side of her face. She wore a white mantilla draped over her shoulders and a crimson skirt tapered at the waist making her stomach bulge. She caught me looking and slapped it down.

'Yes, I must lose some weight,' she laughed, her red mouth revealing a set of sparkling teeth.

Next to her I felt like a small grey mouse.

My mother came in with the tea things, all smiles, and I helped lay them out.

'Tell me, Margaret, what's it like living so far away

in Spain, d'you not get lonely at times? Imagine your father letting you go away like that, he must miss you a lot.'

'Not at all, Mrs O'Dea, he loves it. Now that I'm out of the way he has the house to himself, and can have all the women in he wants.'

My mother tittered politely behind her hand, shielding her false teeth. 'Oh, Margaret, there's no doubt but you're a caution.' She thought Mags was joking.

'Can I give you a hand?' Mags asked my mother when she saw her getting up.

'Not at all, dear, you just sit there and chat. I wouldn't dream of letting you near my kitchen wearing those nice clothes.'

'How've you been apart from your old man dying?' Mags asked after she left. She eyed me and I felt mortified by the clothes I had on. A skirt made out of an old dress of Celine's and an ancient blouse with a Peter Pan collar.

'That outfit does nothing for you if you don't mind me saying.'

'I know, but I've nothing else, there's no money . . .'

'I can lend you some clothes,' she butted in generously. 'And if you smartened up a bit we could go out on a double date together. I met these really nice blokes at the wedding and, guess what, they're rich.' She slapped my knee with glee.

'Thanks, but I'm not interested,' I said and told her about Clair. How crazy I was about him, how there'd never be anyone else.

'So, where is he? When are you going to introduce us?' She looked around as if I was hiding him somewhere.

'He'd to go to London,' I said.

'How long is he gone?'

'A month.'

'How is he getting on?'

'I don't know.' I shook my head and, to my shame, tears welled up.

'You mean he hasn't written?' She put her eyes up to heaven.

I shook my head again.

'You'll meet plenty of those along the way. What's the point in being miserable when he's probably out having a ball. Why don't you get out and enjoy yourself, for Chrissake?'

My mother must have been listening as she came in and said, 'I'm glad you're here to talk some sense into her, Margaret. That's exactly what I think. But if I were to say anything like that she'd eat the face off me.'

I gave her daggers looks which she ignored and asked if I'd fetch the teapot like a dear.

They were talking in low voices when I got back, I heard my mother say: '. . . never liked the sound of him myself.' Her voice rose when she saw me. 'Ah there you are, Marian, now we can have a nice cup of tea.'

She was all charm and buttering up to Mags like mad. I hated it and remembered the great time I had once with the Hansons up the mountains. We'd gone for a long hike, had our picnic by a stream, caught a load of tadpoles and then had a rolling competition down a hill. On the way back Mr Hanson said it was dangerous, but for a treat, he'd turn his engine off. We held our breaths as the car freewheeled down the mountain roads at breakneck speed.

We were so late getting back Mr Hanson came in to explain to my mother. It was a very long drive but I'd been so eager to go with them and didn't seem to want to come back. He laughed and my mother joined in. She was all over him at the door. Thank you again, Mr Hanson. We said goodbye all smiles. But then when the door closed she shook me like a rat.

'How dare you ingratiate yourself with those people in order to get asked out everywhere. The cheek, have you no shame. As for freewheeling the car down the mountain they only did that to save petrol, they're so bloody mean.' She went on, working herself up into a rage until my father came and rescued me, but the day had been ruined.

'Wake up, Marian.' My mother nudged me. 'You're lost to the world. Pass the tea around and look after your friend.'

'Don't worry, Mrs O'Dea, I can look after myself,' Mags said helping herself to a slice of cake.

But my mother kept on. 'Just remember, Marian, it never hurt anyone to put on a pleasant face.'

'I can't change the way my face is made,' I told her angrily.

'No, but one can always improve on nature. Isn't that so, Margaret.' She turned to Mags and asked what her plans were after her year in Spain was up.

'Oh, I don't know, Mrs O'Dea, I'll probably find some rich man to marry me and settle down,' Mags said winking at me.

My mother smiled encouragingly. 'You shouldn't have much difficulty there, Margaret, a good-looking girl like you who knows how to make the best of herself. Life is what you make it, I always say.'

She chatted away with Mags like an old friend till Mags said she had to go. I saw her out to the gate.

'Don't forget, I'll be in touch about the date.'

I knew I couldn't go out with anyone but Clair, but said I'd see.

'Don't be so pathetic, of course you'll come. What you need is a bit of fun.'

We said goodbye, and I watched her totter down the road in her high heels, her full figure wiggling from side to side. Next to her, my body was slight, like a boy's.

'You'll never make a lady out of that one,' was my mother's verdict when I went to help with the washing up. 'Did you smell the perfume? It was bottled on to her.'

'What do you mean, I thought you liked her. You were all over her a minute ago.'

'I had to, she's a friend of yours. But I don't admire your taste. Too forward and brassy by half.'

A tiny bit of me agreed with her, but I couldn't bear to hear her say anything against Mags. I tried to explain what a tough life she had. With her mother and brother dying, she practically had to bring herself up. The way her father was hardly ever there and yet she always put on a brave face and smiled.

'You might take a lesson from her book and be grateful for what you have,' my mother said.

Chapter 21

Celine was having nightmares and kept waking us up with her screams. One night I nearly died when I heard her tear her nails down the wallpaper over and over again. My mother went in to calm her down, wondering what had got into her. She thought it must be worms. She'd give her a good dose in the morning.

The next day Celine slashed her black taffeta to bits with a knife. She said it didn't suit her any more even though she'd worn it only once to a hunt ball with Chard. My mother thought it might have done for me but we never said so.

We didn't dare mention Chard's name. He was supposed to have got in touch after the funeral, but she never heard from him again. My mother said she'd made a faux pas there, and what a fool she was to let him go. What did they expect, I wondered. Celine had always treated Chard like dirt. Strangely enough though my mother seemed to thrive on it. Whenever she mentioned how badly Celine behaved towards Chard, her face went all serious, but her eyes were alive with excitement. She decided Celine needed someone to talk to, someone intellectual to take her out of herself.

'What about that Jesuit you met at the retreat?' she asked. I wasn't keen but she went ahead and rang him all the same and he agreed to come.

The day Father Brian was due, my mother fussed about the kitchen wondering what food to serve. In the end she decided on a mixed grill. It was a safe bet, it wouldn't spoil and all men loved meat.

Celine was in the drawing room surrounded by her props. Dressed in black and heavily made up, she sat smoking through a long mother-of-pearl holder. Her album of photos and press cuttings lay open before her. The Record Cup and her array of medals, polished that morning by my mother, shone down from the piano. Michael MacLiammoir's rich, mournful voice intoned from the record player. 'Out,' she screamed when she saw me and, picking up a script, flung it at the door.

I escaped upstairs, as I didn't feel like seeing anyone, especially Father Brian. Clair hadn't written and I was going insane. He'd probably got a job by now and met someone else. Some beautiful brainy architect like himself. There were sure to be lots over there where it's free to go to university. Not like here, where only the boys get a chance to go. Though it wouldn't make any difference in my case. I hadn't the brains.

I blushed, remembering the time Clair showed me a little model of a building he'd made and I asked like a fool had he always wanted to be an architectural. Architect, he'd said with a smile.

'Marian, there's someone to see you,' my mother called upstairs.

For a moment I'd the wild notion that it might be Clair. My heart leapt as the bedroom door opened until I saw Father Brian standing there. His lips shone with grease from the meal my mother had just served. He raised his hand in a kind of blessing.

'Ah, there you are, Marian. How pleasant to see you again, but what a pity it has to be at such an unhappy time for you and your family. As I have been explaining to your mother and sister your father has gone to a far better place.'

I said nothing and remembered the frog.

'Is this an antique?' he asked, picking a white porcelain dancer off the mantelpiece.

'I dunno, it's nice though.'

His fleshy hands enveloped the piece. I wished he'd put it down. It'd been a present from my father. I remembered he'd given it to me when I'd had the measles. I tried to picture his face but it wouldn't come. I panicked, realising I'd never see him again, he'd gone for ever. Pain struck my heart and rushed to my throat. The tears came. I tried to stop them, but it was no use.

'There, there, now, child.' Father Brian set the figure down and put his arm around me. 'Try and remember, Marian, that this world is but a transient place. And that God made us not just to love and serve him in this life, but to be happy with him for ever in the next. Your father hasn't really died. His immortal soul lives on. If he took good care of it in this life he'll reap his reward with God in the next.'

'How would he take care of it?'

'Take care of what?'

'His soul.'

'How?' Father Brian looked surprised. 'Don't you remember your Catechism, Marian? To save our souls we must worship God through Faith, Hope and Charity.'

'Suppose he didn't look after his soul?'

'Then you must help him now with your prayers and good works. Why don't we kneel down this very minute and say a prayer together.'

To my embarrassment he knelt down on the lino and began to pray:

'O God, the Creator and Redeemer of all mankind, grant to the soul of thy recently departed servant Laurence O'Dea, the remission of all his sins . . .'

He droned on. I stopped listening and thought how crazy it all sounded. Recently departed to where? I couldn't believe he'd gone anywhere but in the ground. And what was his immortal soul anyway? There's only his memory that'll live on and I'll never forget that. Who else had ever cared for me? Clair? But he's gone now. I couldn't see with the sudden tears and hated to cry in front of Father Brian.

He noticed me crying and got up. 'My poor child.' He put his arm around me and sat beside me on the bed. 'There now. Let it all out. It'll do you good.' His pity made it worse. My chest heaved with sobs.

'What you need is a change,' he said stroking my arm gently. 'New horizons perhaps.'

'I need to get away.'

'You can't leave your mother at a time like this. Anyway, where would you go?'

'London or somewhere. I'll get a job.'

'You're underage. Your mother wouldn't allow it. She'd bring you back. And just think what a trial it would be for her with you away in a foreign city open to temptation. She's mentioned to me how worried she is about that boyfriend of yours. How he might easily get you into trouble.' He met my eyes and looked away.

'Trouble? She never said anything to me.'

I realised his hand was moving under my arm and around to my breast. I shifted slightly and it dropped to my waist.

It reminded me of when I was a kid in the cinema

and a man put his hand on my knee. At first I thought
he'd mistaken it for the armrest and left it there. Then
it started to travel upwards and I had to move to
another seat.

'I could help you with a job,' Father Brian said
and began stroking my arm again. He started telling
me about all his business connections when, to my
surprise, I felt his hand creep up and encircle my
breast completely. I watched as his fingers began to
stroke and caress it. Before I could pull back I noticed
his face turning pink. He began to fidget about uneasily.
Then he stood up and pulled a white handkerchief from
his pocket. I reached for it gratefully thinking it was for
me but he shoved it back in his pocket again.

'I'll use your bathroom if I may,' he said and left the
room quickly.

When he'd gone I wiped my face with a Quickie pad
as my mascara had run, and put on some Touch and
Glow. Father Brian returned smiling.

'You're looking better, Marian. What have you done
to your face?'

'Nothing.'

He pulled up a chair. The hams of his legs sank
outwards when he sat down. He anchored his hands
firmly beneath them. We sat in silence, then one hand
escaped and picked up a book.

'What's this rubbish you're reading?' A startled blonde,
her face half obliterated by a black spider, stared back
at him from the cover.

'It's my mother's.'

'Oh.' He set it down gently and asked was I reading
anything?

I mentioned *Dubliners*, a book Clair lent me.

'Ah, Joyce. What did you make of it?'

'It was nice,' I said trying to remember. So much had happened since then. Though one story stuck in my mind. It was so sad, about a girl who couldn't bring herself to run away with her lover to America, and left him at the last minute, just as the boat was sailing.

'Nice?' Father Brian stood up in agitation. 'I don't see how you can possibly apply that word to someone like Joyce. Nice? You do use that word rather a lot, don't you. It doesn't adequately describe anything. It's a hopeless word.' He sounded peeved and began pacing the room.

I didn't say anything, wondering what he was getting so het up about. What the hell did I care about the word nice when my life was in ruins. I turned away as my eyes filled again.

'You need taking out of yourself,' Father Brian said coming over to me.

I got up quickly afraid he'd sit next to me.

'How about a few days away somewhere? Howth perhaps. We could have picnics and go swimming.'

'Father,' my mother called up the stairs. 'Your car's at the door.'

He glanced at his watch. 'I must go. Evening devotions. I'll make arrangements in a week or so. God bless.'

I nodded, wondering did he think I came down with the last shower?

My mother came in beaming. 'Well, that was a great success. Celine's in much better form. You could see he was taken by her. Did you see the big car he went off in? Don't tell me the clergy haven't money. They're loaded.' She went over to the window to settle the curtains. 'My God, would you look at the filth of these, he must have seen them.' She yanked them back. 'Spring cleaning will

162

have to begin in earnest next week.' She smiled. 'It's good to have a priest in the house at a time like this and he's such a nice man, so intelligent, knows everything about the theatre. They're forbidden to go, you know. Only allowed in to dress rehearsals. He's going to call regularly from now on. Isn't that nice?'

'Well, I'm not in next time he calls,' I said.

'Now don't you start, Marian. Haven't I enough to contend with, what with that one downstairs and your Daddy not yet cold in his grave.'

She left the room, banging the door behind her.

Chapter 22

My father hadn't made a will so the shop automatically went to my mother and Uncle Ted. They couldn't keep it on as they hated each other's guts so it had to be sold.

When all the furniture in the shop disappeared overnight my mother said Uncle Ted and his crowd were plotting against her. She was worried sick as we'd always lived on credit and had bills owing all over the place. Some were long overdue and there wasn't money enough in the bank even to cover the funeral.

Then a job came up in the Asylum. The matron needed an assistant to look after the laundry and uniforms. My mother applied as she was good at sewing. She owned a treadle Singer sewing machine. Once she went so fast on the pedal the needle went straight through her finger and out the other side.

My mother hadn't worked since she was married. The only other two women in the Avenue who worked were both widows. One of them, a civil servant, had her parents in to live with her. She'd two sets of twins, all identical. They were never allowed out to play. We always stopped and watched when they passed down our road, dressed the same like a family of clones.

The other widow was a dressmaker with three daughters and five sons. She worked at home and had someone in to help with the dressmaking. She

165

Miriam Dunne

did very well, making outfits for most of the neighbourhood. The mystery was how they all managed to live there, as the two downstairs rooms were taken up with the dressmaking business. Her youngest threw himself out the bedroom window once. He landed in the rockery. It was a miracle he didn't kill himself. My mother said it was due to overcrowding.

My mother got the asylum job. No one else wanted it because of the fear of being attacked by the inmates. I was terrified for her but my mother didn't seem to mind. I'll be all right, she assured me, and it'll get me out of the house. I told her to remember that the inmates weren't just insane. Most of them were convicted criminals.

She was given a heavy set of keys which she had to carry with her everywhere. The one thing they insisted on was that every door had to be locked behind you. It took ages, she said, as the building was a warren of rooms. She thought the inmates were harmless. More like children really. Some of them went round thinking they were famous people. There was Florence Nightingale, Napoleon and Alexander the Great. You were safe as long as you got their names right. Napoleon was her favourite, such a gentleman. He always got up when she entered a room. He obviously knows I'm a lady, she laughed. And the way he stood there all day, with his hand tucked inside his waistcoat, lost in another world, no trouble to anyone.

My mother loved working there. She enjoyed the company and seemed almost happy for once. The matron liked her as she got through a mountain of sewing. She was a favourite with the inmates, and spoilt them with her little treats of homemade cakes and buns. She even got some of their headed notepaper for me which I wanted as a souvenir. I sent a few letters off to some friends. I even sent one to Mother Borgia.

Central Criminal Lunatic Asylum,
Dundrum Road,
Dublin

Dear Mother Borgia,

    As you can see from my address, since leaving L.A.D. a little over a year ago, things have gone from bad to worse.

    I am desperately trying to pull my socks up but they keep filling up with ants.

    Assuring you of our best attention at all times,

      Yours faithfully,

      Marian O'Dea

P.S. They've taken away my toothbrush.

One day I nearly had a fit when my mother arrived home from the asylum. She stumbled in the door with her glasses smashed and an ugly swelling over one eye. Napoleon had punched her. He'd been going round with his hands in his pockets and she'd called him Wellington by mistake.

It wasn't the same for my mother after that. She took most of the work home with her and only went to the asylum when it was absolutely necessary. I had warned her they were dangerous, but then my mother always was the best judge of character.

Chapter 23

There was still no word from Clair. Mags rang to say she'd been sorting through her clothes and there were some that she thought might suit me. Her family had moved while she was away and she gave me her new address. It was somewhere in Goatstown. She warned me to keep a good eye out as the name on the gate was worn with age.

The size of the house bowled me over when it came into view through the overgrown drive. I stopped to take it all in. Two weather-beaten columns framed the entrance with a pair of double doors. A row of giant windows flanked them on either side looking as if they'd take a week to open and another week to close. The only thing that jarred was a flashy red Triumph parked outside the door.

I pressed the bell and heard it ring far away. Mags opened the door holding a hanky to her chin. She looked out of place in tight pants, waspie and a black polo neck.

'You never told me you lived in such an old house.'

'Yeah, it's falling apart like myself. Look at this.' She removed her hanky and showed me a large pimple underneath. 'My skin's desperate since I came home.'

'Leave it alone, don't touch it,' I advised.

We went through to the entrance hall where four rooms in our house could easily fit.

'Why did your father buy such a big place when there's only the two of you?' I asked, green with envy as I loved old houses.

'He met these people in a pub who were going on about this old ruin they'd seen, so he went out and bought it straight away.'

I followed her downstairs, through a long passageway into a vast kitchen with a range running the length of the room.

'D'you want coffee? There's water on. I was just going to steam my face.'

'No, you carry on.'

She had water boiling on top of a small portable stove. It looked as if they were camping out.

'Can I have a look around?' I asked amazed by a row of numbered bells dangling over the door.

'Work away. He bought it as an investment. He thinks it's going to make his fortune when he does it up.'

We heard a noise upstairs.

'Is that him?' I asked.

'No, he's never here. It's Eddie. He's on the roof sunbathing.'

'Who's Eddie?'

'The one I was telling you about, we met at the wedding. His friend Mick's coming later.'

My heart sank. I thought we'd the place to ourselves.

She eyed my clothes. 'Go up and see if you can find anything to wear. There's a pile on the floor inside my bedroom door.'

She told me where to go and showed me the stairs. There were two. I chose the main one that swept upwards and around to a long corridor of rooms. An elegant alcove at the top housed a family of wellington boots. Mags's room, beside the bathroom, had only a mattress on the floor, a couple of chairs and a huge mausoleum of a wardrobe. I rooted through her clothes hoping I'd find something that would suit. They all looked too fussy. Mags could get away with flashy gold trimmings, Lurex and glitter, but it made me look like a Christmas tree. I found a fitted skirt and pale gold top that might do.

Excited by something new to wear, I stripped off and tried them on in front of the mirror inside her wardrobe door. The skirt wasn't bad if I moved the buttons and the top went well with my blonde hair.

Footsteps in the corridor made me freeze. They paused outside the door and went on into the bathroom. Then someone started pissing like a horse. At first I thought they'd turned on the bath, but then I heard the toilet flush and a ferocious stream of farts. Without thinking I climbed into the wardrobe and closed the door. A row of metal coathangers chimed softly above as I nestled into Mags's clothes. They smelt faintly of stale perfume and sweat.

Without warning someone came into the room. I held my breath as they made straight for the wardrobe and opened the door. I shrank back and watched through the folds of a skirt as Eddie, for it must have been him, examined himself in the mirror.

All he had on were shoes and socks and a pair of flesh-coloured bathing trunks. He was too busy admiring himself to notice me there. His back, burnt mahogany brown, looked odd compared to the front of him which was stark white. Standing with feet apart and shoulders hunched, he flexed his muscles and a self-satisfied grin slowly spread across his face revealing his buckteeth. He reminded me of an ape.

Mags's voice boomed up from downstairs. 'What are yous all doing up there? Mick's arrived.'

The wardrobe door closed and Eddie disappeared. I waited for his footsteps to die away before climbing out.

The sun was streaming through the large windows spotlighting the rising dust. Outside an overgrown field with willow trees swept down to a lake. I tried to imagine what it was like long ago, with hordes of servants to run the place. The house had a presence of its own which demanded respect. Was it because it had lived so long and seen so many things? I couldn't imagine the semis we lived in having the same effect after so many years. They wouldn't gain any dignity with age but would become shabby and depressing-looking even if they lasted that long.

I didn't hear Mags come into the room. 'What the hell d'you think you're doing? The two of them are waiting for us downstairs. Eddie wanted to know was that my kid sister hiding in the wardrobe.'

She was all dolled up in a tight dress and high heels. Her orangey make-up ended at the line of her face and made her look as if she was wearing a mask.

'I don't really want to go,' I said.

'Oh, don't be such a drip. Here, put on some lipstick and you can borrow this.' She handed me her lipstick and compact case and, opening the wardrobe, took out a jacket with a streak of lightning down the back in silver sequins. I wouldn't wear it in a fit and took it just to please her.

They were waiting for us in the car. Mags introduced me and got in front with Eddie. He looked better with his mouth shut and clothes on.

My heart sank when I saw Mick in the back. He wore

a bright blue suit and had bad skin. I could smell his hair oil and a faint whiff of manure.

'Hi,' I said.

He bared his teeth in a smile.

'Where to?' Mags shrieked as we shot off and were flung back in our seats.

'Cliff Castle Hotel and then we'll see . . .' Eddie paused and gave Mags a wink. He squeezed her knee. She slapped him off smiling happily.

'Was that you in the wardrobe?' Eddie asked, glancing back at me.

'Yeah, I was looking for something to wear. How's it your back's so brown and you're stark white in the front?'

'That's what comes from lying on top of Mags all day in the sun.'

They all laughed. Mick sounded like a horse.

'You should see the rest of me sometime,' Eddie grinned and his sharp teeth stuck out a mile. 'What d'you say, Marian?'

They were waiting for me to make some smart remark in return but I was hopeless like that. I knew the more they laughed the more gloomy I'd get. Mags gave me a look. She was pissed off I wouldn't play along.

She turned to Eddie and slapping his thigh told him to haul in his teeth and give us a song. As we flew along the coast road he started up:

'*For rambling or roving or football and sporting*
and drinking black porter as fast as you fill . . .'

They all joined in. I thought of the music Clair played when we made love, 'Round Midnight', and of his long

173

lean body and sensitive hands. My eyes filled and I stared hard out the window. At least they went on singing and we didn't have to talk.

The Cliff Castle Hotel looked out over Killiney Hill. It wasn't a real castle, but made of smooth cement with lines cut in to resemble blocks of stone.

The lounge and dining area with its deep red carpet and soft lights had a subdued air. People sat in groups talking quietly. They looked up startled when we came in and Eddie's voice boomed, 'This is a dead duck of a place till after eleven. What'll yous have?'

'We're off to the powder room, boys, we'll be back in a sec,' Mags said, sounding like a little girl.

'Tell us what you're having before you go, we're gasping.' Eddie signalled to a waiter and sat down at a corner table with Mick.

Mags wanted a Club Orange with ice. I asked for Club Lemon.

Eddie turned to Mick. 'What's yours? A Club foot?'

They all laughed. Mags nearly got hysterical and had to be thumped on the back. I smiled. It wasn't that funny, I thought. Eddie looked pleased and persuaded Mags to have a vodka with her orange.

'Just to please you,' she said doing her dumb bit again. I said I was off to the loo. Mags followed me, she looked really annoyed, you wouldn't think she was laughing her head off a moment ago. When we went into the Ladies she turned on me.

'For God's sake, liven up, will you. What's the matter with you?'

'I dunno, I can't help it. I keep thinking of Clair.'

'Oh for Chrissake, you're not going to see him again, take it from me.' She inspected her spot in the mirror and, taking out her Panstick make-up, applied another layer. She offered me some, but I refused. 'There's Mick out there large as life, concentrate on him.'

'He's not my type, Mags.'

'I'm not asking you to marry him. Just go out there and enjoy yourself. Laugh, have a good time.' She got out her lipstick and rouge. 'At least put on some rouge. You look like death warmed up.' She dabbed some on my cheeks.

I rubbed it off and said I'd better go home.

'You can't leave now, they're buying us dinner and taking us out. If you walk out now I'll never speak to you again.'

'But we haven't had anything yet,' I protested.

'No, but Eddie will have ordered. We always have steak medium rare. What do you think of him?' she asked, twisting around to see if her bra straps showed at the back.

'I don't really know him.'

'He's a bit of gas once he gets going. Can you see my straps?'

'No, they're OK. Do you love him?' I asked.

'Jesus, Marian, I don't know. He's rolling in it, that'll do for a start.'

'Would you marry him?'

'He hasn't asked me yet.'

'No, but would you?' I realised she'd marry him tomorrow if he asked and love had nothing to do with it.

'Why not, I could do worse. C'mon, let's go, for Chrissake, or they'll have found someone else.'

I wish to God they would, I thought.

'What does Eddie do?' I asked on the way back.

'He's a bookie. Why?'

'Nothing, just wondered. How about Mick?'

'He's a pig farmer, don't laugh.'

I wasn't going to, but that explained the whiff of manure.

Mags put on her big smile before she opened the door and went back in to join them. Eddie had his arm around a waitress. When he saw us coming he dropped it and let it rest on the back of his chair.

'There you are, girls. I've ordered the steaks. Mick and I are having oxtail soup, anyone else?'

'No thanks,' we both said.

Mags flopped down beside Eddie. The waitress took his menu away. Mick kept his, he was studying it intently and didn't look up when I sat next to him. Eddie held up a roll of notes. 'By the way, Mags, you won again this afternoon. Twenty to one on Rambling Rose.'

Mags let out a shriek and threw her arms around him.

'We'll make a gambler of you yet. As long as you've got me to give you the tips.'

Mags beamed as he took her bag and dropped the money in. Then he rummaged around till he found her lipstick. Mags pretended to object, but you could see she liked the way he was fooling around.

Eddie clumsily removed the top of her lipstick and began twisting it slowly up and down. He kept rolling his eyes while he was doing it and made kissing sounds. Mick sniggered behind the menu and Mags laughed out loud.

'Sister Marian doesn't approve,' said Eddie.

Luckily, the waitress came up then with the soup. Eddie and Mick drained their pints and ordered two more. Mags agreed to another vodka and orange. I asked for some water.

'A pint or a glass?' Eddie wanted to know. He put his hand over his mouth and asked Mags in a loud whisper: 'Does Marian think it's still Lent or what?'

Mags told him to quit messing and get on with his soup.

'Are you looking forward to going back to Spain?' I said to her.

'Are you joking me? I hate it over there. They treat me like shit and the kids are brats. But I've signed a contract and have to see the year out.'

Mick asked me to pass him the pepper and salt. It was the first time he'd spoken. When he started his soup, he made such a loud noise slurping it up that I thought he was doing it for a joke. It was the funniest thing I'd heard all day and I was just about to laugh when I realised the others hadn't noticed. It dawned on me that he always ate like that.

'Let's in on the joke,' Eddie said looking at me.

'It's nothing.'

'Yeah, c'mon, that's the rule. Everyone has to tell a joke when they come out with us.'

'I can never remember jokes,' I said.

'No excuse, you had one there a minute ago.'

'No, I've only got a story, sitting here reminded me of it. It's not really a joke . . .'

'For Chrissake, get on with it,' Mags said twisting her hair around fast.

'It's about an old woman who came from the mountains where it was a sign of poverty not to have any teeth,' I explained. 'Her daughter married well and bought her a set of false teeth, but she couldn't wear them as they hurt too much. When she was taken to a restaurant for a treat she couldn't bear to let people think she was too poor to have any teeth. So she always brought them with her and left them sitting on the tablecloth beside her so people would know she wasn't hard up.'

There was silence when I finished. The waitress came and cleared away the plates.

'Was that a joke?' Eddie asked.

'No, not really.'

'I think it's disgusting,' said Eddie. 'It'd put anyone off their dinner.'

Just then the steaks arrived and Mags quickly started telling some rigmarole of a joke about an Irishman, an Englishman, and a Scotsman.

I didn't listen and watched Mick tucking into his steak as if he could never get enough. He was as tall as Clair, but weedy, like a plant that had bolted for the light but never filled out.

I offered him my steak.

'Are you sure?' He looked surprised.

'Yeah,' I said and slid it on to his plate. I couldn't eat it. The sight of it oozing with blood put me off.

'What's wrong with the steak?' Eddie wanted to know.

'Nothing, has anyone a penny?' I asked.

Eddie rooted in his pocket. 'It's not Friday you know, Marian, you can eat it.'

'I know,' I said and went past him. He caught my hand and pressed a penny into my palm. He held it there. I pulled away.

'Are you going to light a candle for me?' he asked.

'No, you're past it,' I said and went off.

I locked myself in the loo. Even though it hurt I wanted to think about Clair. I had to, it was like a sore you kept picking at until it was raw. Mags was probably right. I'd never see him again. It was over six weeks now since he'd left. He must have started a new life by now and met someone else. Look at the way he got off with the girl at the party that night, I reminded myself. He'd asked me to go, but I went to confession instead, and he went by himself. Some girl came up to him in the middle of it and laid her head in his lap. They ended up in bed together. If he was like that when we were apart for only one night, what would he be like in London after six weeks?

Mags burst into the loo to say we were going for a spin.

'I have to go home,' I told her.

'We'll go straight home afterwards,' she promised. 'Anyway, it's impossible to get home on your own from here. You'd have to walk miles.'

Mick was waiting by the door.

'Where's Eddie?' Mags wanted to know.

Mick nodded to the reception area where Eddie was talking to the waitress. He slipped something into her hand.

'Eddie, we're here,' Mags called in a loud voice.

Eddie came bounding over all smiles. 'Jesus, let's get out of here fast. There's more life in a morgue.'

He held open the glass door as we went out. The waitress came up smiling and waved to Eddie as he left. I noticed her black uniform had turned green under the armpits.

'What was that all about?' Mags wanted to know when we got into the car.

'Just gave her a few tips for Leopardstown tomorrow. She'll pass the word around and they'll all have a little flutter. It's good for business.'

Mags eyed him suspiciously, wondering whether to believe him or not.

We sped off downhill towards the sea. Although it was after nine, the evening was still bright. Giant rhododendrons were coming into bloom along the way.

'Talking about business, how's your old man doing?' Eddie asked Mags. She didn't answer. He seemed oblivious to her mood and rattled on. 'That house he bought's not bad. The roof's sound. How much did he pay for it?'

'I haven't a clue,' Mags said coldly. Anyone could see she was put out by the way he'd been sucking up to the waitress.

'That's something I wouldn't do in a fit,' Eddie said.

'What?' Mags asked.

'Building. I'd rather be dragged along by a wild horse. But take engines now, or tinkering with cars. That's a different kettle of fish. I could lie under a car for a week.' He pulled into a parking area overlooking the sea.

'What's this, I thought we were going for a spin?' I said.

'D'you mind if we stop for a minute and admire the view?' Eddie asked sarcastically.

If that's all you're doing it'll be fine I thought.

We looked out over a soft blue sea and a beach that stretched for miles. The sun hung suspended over the horizon in a haze of pinks and golds. You could stare at it without going blind. I was thinking how nice it all was when Eddie made a sudden lunge at Mags. She gave a little yelp and then went quiet when he kissed her on the mouth. Yuck, I said to myself, thinking of his sharp protruding teeth.

His head had twisted around so he could see us in

the back. He winked at Mick. I couldn't get out of the car quickly enough.

The beach was deserted. I took off my shoes and stockings and ground my feet in the sand. It felt great until I saw Mick coming. I suppose he couldn't have stayed in the car watching the other two.

'Would you like to skim a stone?' I asked when he came up.

'Let's sit here for a bit first,' he said and lay back on a sand dune.

That'd be fatal I thought and told him I wanted to have a paddle. I walked down to the sea hoping he wouldn't follow. The water was so cold, it numbed my feet. Hitching my skirt up I belted along the shore, putting as much distance as I could between the two of us.

When I came to a little cove I ducked behind some rocks and sat watching the swell. The tide was on the turn. It crept in, lifting up the seaweed and swirling through the rock pools reviving them after the day's sun.

The sand was damp, perfect for castles. I scooped up a huge heap, made a tunnel through the centre, and built a high wall.

Mick arrived in the middle of it. 'Why did you run off like that?' He sat panting on a nearby rock. 'What are you doing?' he asked.

'What d'you think?'

I sat back to admire my castle wondering what its chances were against the incoming tide. The next thing Mick was on top of me. It was as if he'd fallen off the rock. All the wind was knocked out of me. I couldn't breathe or move anything except for my head. I twisted it from side to side trying to avoid his mouth. He

started fumbling with my skirt and I struggled like a
mad thing.

'Stop it, Mick, get off me for Chrissake. I'm going
with someone else.'

He went limp all of a sudden and I pushed him off.

'What did you come for then?' he asked and got up,
brushing himself down. My castle was in ruins. He'd
rolled over it in the struggle.

'It was Mags's idea.'

'Just like me.'

'What d'you mean?'

'It was Eddie's idea. He thinks I should be going out
with someone my own age.'

'Are you going with anyone?'

'Yeah.'

As we walked back he told me all about this woman
he met through an advertisement in *Ireland's Own*. She
was a widow of forty with a child of ten.

It was dead lonely, he said, since his parents died and
his brothers had all gone off to England and America.
There were hardly any young people left in the area. I
remembered Mags saying he lived in some godforsaken
hole of a place in the country.

'It's like being in a family again when she comes to
my house,' he went on and then added, 'it's not what
people think. Her kid comes too. We have a meal and
play cards. But people talk, it's such a small place. And
Eddie's always harping on her age. It's true enough, she
could be my mother.'

'What d'you listen to Eddie for?' I asked.

'He's a pal of mine. We go drinking together and
racing.'

We'd arrived back at the car. There was no sign of
Eddie and Mags. I felt relieved until I saw the two of

them on top of each other in the back seat. When he saw us Eddie scrambled up and got out, mumbling something about going for a slash.

Mags eased herself up. Her make-up had gone, mascara and all which made her eyes look small. Her face looked squashed. It was as if she'd been in a fight and had barely lasted the course.

Eddie came back doing up his fly. 'Are we right then?' he said getting into the car. We drove off.

'What happened to you two?' Mags asked in a tired voice.

'We went for a walk,' I said.

'How far did you go?' Eddie said with a leer. 'Not as far as us I'd say, what d'you think, Mags?' He laughed. No one else did.

They dropped me off first. 'Good luck with your one,' I called back to Mick and waved goodbye to the others.

I was about to slam the car door when Mags asked, 'Aren't you going to thank Eddie for the evening?'

'Forget it, she's a dead loss,' Eddie said and drove off fast.

Chapter 24

Father Brian called again and caught me unawares. He arrived on the doorstep carrying a brown box and said he wanted to record my voice. My mother thought it strange. Surely he meant Celine? When I told him I couldn't, my mother said nonsense, of course you can, and invited him in for tea and scones.

He set the recorder up on the drawing-room floor and showed me how it worked. I hunkered down to watch. He asked me to say something meaningful into it. I said I'd try if he left me on my own. As we stood up he remarked on my height. I was taller than expected, he said, considering my legs were quite short from the knees down. They must be much longer from the knees up. He thought that was interesting in a girl of my age.

At first I couldn't think of anything to say except 'hello, hello' and make galloping sounds with my fingers. Then I recited that corny poem about a mother's love, where the boy at his evil mistress's command kills his mother and takes her heart to feed her hungry hounds. As he runs through the night he falls and the heart lying beside him on the ground asks softly, 'Are you hurt, my child, are you hurt at all?'

I didn't know what Father Brian would make of it, but it always left me in bits. This time I couldn't help crying.

It all seemed so hopeless with Clair gone and my father dead. Even Clair's jumper which I took to bed with me every night had been found by my mother and washed so thoroughly there wasn't a trace left of his smell.

I was lying on the floor, deaf from the tears running into my ears when Father Brian walked in. He was about to kneel down, but this time I jumped up and pretended I'd a cold.

'You're very agitated all of a sudden,' he complained. 'It's probably after the death and everything. I hope you're not pining for that boyfriend who left you at such a difficult time. It's all to the good you know, Marian. He was an occasion of sin for you and best forgotten.'

He began to pack away his things and reminded me of our trip to Howth and had I got a swimming costume. He thought a complete break away from it all for at least a week might be best. He'd some leave coming up, he'd speak to my mother about it.

I told him it was impossible. We'd no money. I had to find work. He said that could easily be arranged with all his business connections. I tried to tell him I hadn't any qualifications but he wouldn't listen. 'That's not important. It's not what you know, it's who you know.' As he spoke he tried to touch my chest as if to make a point but I kept moving out of range.

He finally sat down and clasped his hands together. They reminded me of a bunch of bananas. 'I'll ring around and fix up a few interviews for you.'

'What for?' I asked carelessly.

'I don't know yet, but it's good to get out and meet people. There may not be anything for you at the moment, but they'll keep you in mind and put you on file. You've done a commercial course. That's a very useful thing to have. Be sure and mention it at the interviews.'

I thought of Miss Boyle's classes and the secretarial exam and told him it was no use. I could barely type, my shorthand was disastrous and I couldn't spell.

'You've a good voice though. If you cultivated the right manner and presented yourself well you could answer the phone. I know someone in Packaging, a Mr Ward. He's the Managing Director, a very important man. They often have a vacancy.'

'Packaging, what's that?'

'Containers, packets, you must know what I mean. When you think about it everything needs packaging nowadays. It's a growth industry. They're even talking about doing away with milk bottles and replacing them with cartons. Much more hygienic and economical, so Mr Ward tells me. Of course the Americans are doing it already. They're streets ahead of us.'

I sat there nodding as he rattled on. I couldn't think of anything more deadly than packaging. I remembered once, when my mother was putting out her empty milk bottles on the windowsill, she forgot to open the window and crashed through the glass splitting her hand open. All because she didn't want to go outside and let Gertie see her in her dressing gown and curlers.

'He's a fine man, Mr Ward. Very generous to the Church,' Father Brian said, getting up at last. He gathered up his recording machine. 'God bless, Marian. I'll be in touch about our little holiday.'

After he left I thought, why not take a job if I was offered one? If I saved up enough I might be able to go over and see Clair. But suppose he wasn't interested any more? He hadn't written and I didn't even know his address. It reminded me of the story of this orphan who went over to see her boyfriend in England only to find him with someone else. She hadn't a penny, knew no one, and had to spend the night on the floor with the two of them at it all night in the bed. It was during the Satanic anti-God Campaign in England and everyone said her mother must have interceded for her in Heaven as she'd been given a return ticket by mistake and was able to get back to Ireland the next day.

Celine was offered a job in Butlins working as a Redcoat. Between that and her work in the Gate my mother was thrilled. If only you could do as well, she kept on till one day Father Brian rang to say he'd got me an interview. She was all over him on the phone. I sat listening on the stairs. When she came to tell me I asked her what it was for?

'How should I know? Go and ask him yourself and get a move on. No priest should be kept waiting for the likes of you.' She sounded so vicious. It was hard to believe she was the same charmer who'd just spoken to him a minute ago.

Father Brian didn't know either. He just told me where to go and to ask for a Mr Hare. The interview was for ten. For some reason I didn't leave enough time to get there and had to run all the way from D'Olier Street to way up past the Rotunda.

The girl in reception looked startled when I burst in red-faced and out of breath. She directed me to a waiting room full of girls who looked as if they'd just stepped out of *Vogue*. Is this a modelling agency? I wondered, and felt miserable knowing I looked a hick in my mother's swing back coat and an old pair of Celine's slip-ons. The conversation stopped for a moment as they eyed me, scrutinising my clothes. Their expressions said – surely you've come to the wrong place? I flicked through a magazine pretending to read. The girl opposite had her hair in a beehive adding inches to her height. I remembered when the style came out first. The dire warnings that went around when someone left hers up for a month and found a nest of insects had settled in.

They all seemed to know each other. One started moaning about her figure. She only had to look at a cream cake to put on weight. PLJ and a banana diet was recommended. A blonde girl complained that lacquer dulled her hair, but how else could she keep it in place? Someone suggested rubbing in a raw egg before the final rinse, and then when it was dry, polishing it with a piece of silk. Wouldn't the hot water curdle the egg? I wondered, when my name was called.

Mr Hare sat round-faced and bald behind a framed motto which read:

GENIUS IS AN INFINITE CAPACITY FOR TAKING PAINS

He waved me to a seat while the receptionist handed him some papers and whispered in his ear. I heard Father Brian's name mentioned and blushed, remembering what he'd said. 'It's not what you know. It's who you know.' I thought it unfair, surely the job should go to whoever's best.

When the receptionist left, Mr Hare started asking a load of questions. Before he could mention exams I told him I hadn't done any. I had to leave school when my mother got ill.

'Is she all right now?' he asked with a look of surprise.

I nodded, and was about to mention my father's death but thought better not. He said he'd a daughter my age still at school.

'Really,' I said trying to sound interested.

'Do you wear a hat?' he suddenly asked.

'No.'

'Never?'

'Well, only a scarf at Mass.'

He smiled and stood up. We shook hands, he thanked me for coming and said he'd be in touch. It was only when I was halfway down the road I realised I'd forgotten to ask what the job was for.

My mother was just finishing her tea when I got home. 'What kept you? You've been gone all day,' she wanted to know.

'Nothing. I just wandered around, didn't feel like coming home.'

'And why not? Is your home not good enough for you?' She sounded peeved.

'Any news?' I asked pouring myself a cup.

'My left ear's been burning all day, someone must be talking about me. Hope it's good,' she said putting on her coy look.

I hated when she went on like this, acting like a little girl.

'Imagine,' she said. 'Both my girls working. Now I can retire in peace.'

'What are you talking about?'

'Father Brian was here. He was on to that man you went to see. He says they were very impressed.'

'Rubbish,' I snapped.

My mother looked shocked. 'Priests never lie, Marian. I'm surprised at you.'

I let it go, and waited for her to go on.

'Anyway, he told me to tell you you've got the job if you get your hair done and wear black.'

'What's the job?' I asked knowing I'd only got it because of him.

'Modelling hats,' my mother smirked. 'Imagine that, you who's never worn a hat,' she laughed.

I thought it unfair; it should have gone to one of the other girls.

The job was to start the following week at an hotel down by the Quays where buyers from all over the country came to view the new season's collection.

'By the way, Father Brian wants to take you to Howth for a few days before you start,' my mother went on. 'I think it's very kind and thoughtful of him to take such an interest. He's left you money to buy clothes for the job. It's only a loan mind, but really decent of him, I thought.' She nodded to the sideboard where some notes lay tucked under a mat. 'I hope you'll find some way to repay him for all his kindness.'

Chapter 25

'Was there any post?' I asked my mother next morning at breakfast.

'No. Were you expecting something?' she said, beheading her boiled egg. 'Who from? I hope it's not that arrogant pup you were going out with?' She scooped out the top and laid it aside. 'Good riddance to him, I said to myself when he took himself off.'

I couldn't believe what she was saying and turned on her in a rage. 'How can you say that about someone you don't even know?'

'He rang one day when you were out. I could tell by his tone. I said to myself, that one sounds too sure of himself by half . . .'

'What d'you mean his *tone*? How can you judge someone from their *tone*. You've never even seen him!' I was yelling by now. She seemed so stupid and thick I couldn't bear the way she went on, running people down. 'How is it you never have a good word to say about men. As for my father . . . !'

'What about him?'

'You never gave a damn about him. Why on earth did you marry him?'

'My mother thought it was time I settled down.'

'Weren't you in love with him?'

'Love?' She suddenly looked lost like a child who

didn't know what I was talking about. She might have had a glimmer once but it was long gone.

She recovered herself and said in a fluster. 'Don't talk about things you don't understand. You're too young for all that.'

How old did you have to be to know about love, I wondered.

'When did you first meet?' I asked.

'Who?'

'My father of course.'

'My mother introduced us. She was a good customer of his,' she said reluctantly.

So it was her mother who arranged it, I thought.

'But your mother never liked him, you've always told me that.'

She drained the pot and, covering it with the cosy, stared out the window. 'You may not believe it to look at me now, Marian, but there was a time when I could have married anyone.'

'Why didn't you? What stopped you?' I added sarcastically.

'You don't know the half of it. What I've had to put up with all these years. It's more than just your father,' she added quickly, seeing I was about to butt in. 'It was before that. I can't explain.'

'Why not?' I kept on, but she turned away and said nothing.

'Was it to do with our brother? My father said something . . .'

'What?' She spun around, her face strained.

'Nothing really. Neither of you ever wanted to talk about him. I always wondered why he never had a name . . .'

'He wasn't baptised,' she cut in.

'I know, but even so, you don't remember his birth-day or anything.'

'I want to blot all that time out,' she said and staring down at the tablecloth gathered the crumbs that clung to her finger and dropped them neatly on to her sideplate.

'If it hadn't been for my mother and the parish priest I don't know what I'd have done,' she said suddenly. 'That's why I want you to keep in with Father Brian. A priest is a great comfort when you're in trouble.'

'But what about my father, couldn't he help?'

'Him? He was no better than the rest,' she said brushing the rest of the crumbs on to the floor in a sudden fit of anger. 'Pestering you night and day. They're all the same, the lot of them with their dirty minds . . .'

She went on working herself up into her usual rage about men only being after the one thing. I'd heard it all before and knew it was useless to interrupt. It only made her worse. When she finished we sat in silence.

I tried again. 'My father mentioned there was some-one else.'

'When?' she asked irritably.

I waited, hoping she'd tell me herself. How she'd nearly drowned. Who had pulled her out? Everything. But I couldn't ask her outright because I'd promised my father.

'I might have known he wouldn't keep his mouth shut,' she said bitterly. She went quiet for a minute and then asked, 'Had he drink on him when he started all this reminiscing? Because if he had he was talking through his hat. You wouldn't want to believe a word of it.'

She was getting angry again. I tried to calm her. 'He told me he always felt second best.'

'Well, he didn't do too badly out of it. Everyone said how well he looked after he married me. With all the home cooking. He was nothing before I married him. Living in squalor over the shop with that brother of his. The both of them well into their forties. He never knew what it was like to have a proper home till he met me.'

'A proper home. Is that what you call it? I'd rather have been born over the wall in the asylum.'

'That's where you'll end up if you're not careful.'

'No, that's where Celine will end up if you're not careful.'

'What did you say?' She turned on me in a rage.

'You know she's half bats and it's got out of hand. You can't control her.'

'There's nothing wrong with Celine,' my mother said firmly. 'Everyone thinks very highly of her.'

'Only the people who don't know her. She can fool them easily enough. Why do you think she's an actress?'

'I don't know. Why do you keep picking on me?'

'What about the other night when she had the fit. Is that normal?'

'She was upset that's all.'

'Upset?' I said in disbelief.

Celine had come home that night in a rage and lit into my mother. I was in bed when I heard shouting and went to listen on the stairs. They hadn't renewed her contract at the Gate. She was convinced it was because some bastard of a critic gave her a bad review in her last play. She played the part of a maid and the reviewer had mentioned that there was 'too much dusting going on'. As if anyone cared or even noticed, I thought.

My mother tried to calm her by saying how lucky it was she had the Redcoat job to fall back on. There was an almighty crash. Celine had hurled the iron at my mother. Luckily it missed and crashed into the Crinoline Lady fire screen instead. I heard shuffling and ran down. Celine was attacking my mother. They were wrestling by the fireplace. My mother tried to ward off her blows and was treading on the broken glass in her slippers. I let out a scream, caught hold of Celine's hair and dragged her away. She ran upstairs slamming doors after her.

Later that night I woke up and heard her prowling around the house muttering. There was no key in my door and I was terrified she'd come in and attack me. In the end I got under the bed with my pillow and eiderdown.

Someone rang her the next day. We listened with relief as she told whoever it was that she'd been released by the Gate for the summer and was going to work in Butlins as a Redcoat.

We had started clearing away the breakfast things when my mother brought up Clair again.

'Now, what about this person Clair, Marian? I know he's not right for you. I've met his type before. Clair? What sort of name is that for a boy, anyway?'

'I don't want to talk about it.'

'Mark my words, Marian. I'm never wrong.'

'Well, you were wrong once,' I said angry with her for having another go at Clair. 'So wrong it nearly killed you.'

She turned away as if she'd been struck and made no answer.

I went upstairs thinking how lucky it was Clair and my mother never met. She would have hated him on sight. And he would have seen through her straight away. The way he saw through Celine the first time they met.

Celine and my mother were always taken in by appearances. If I brought home a boyfriend, it wouldn't matter if he was a mass murderer as long as he was well dressed and said all the right things. When I'd moaned about the few clothes I had once Clair said, 'It's what's inside that counts.'

That night I kept going over the time my mother nearly drowned. I tried to imagine what it would be like if Clair did that to me. It didn't bear thinking about. Until then I'd always pictured my mother in her finery stepping on to a boat with lots of people around. When she missed her footing and fell into the sea I imagined everyone lending a hand to help pull her out. I thought she was only angry with some man for not coming to her aid quickly enough.

But it wasn't like that. There was only the two of them. She was pregnant and couldn't swim. While she struggled in the water he just stood there and watched. She would have drowned if someone hadn't come along. After all that she had to tell her mother she was pregnant and the parish priest was dragged in. My mother was in awe of her own mother. She never said a word against her but by all accounts, she was hardhearted and cruel. No wonder my mother went into raptures whenever she talked about her time in England. The freedom probably went to her head.

For some reason that terrible film I'd seen with Clair came to mind. It was about this woman in Sicily who was raped by a bandit and became pregnant. The child was the image of its father. He adored his mother but she couldn't stand the sight of him anywhere near her.

Chapter 26

It was a bright clear day. The sun streamed through the bedroom windows, curtainless now that my mother had started spring cleaning. All the rugs were up, and the lace runners and covers lay steeping in the bathroom. The house had a bare look, as if we were moving and starting life afresh.

My mother had left Father Brian's money under the glass top on the dressing table for safe keeping.

'Be sure now and only buy a black rig-out for the job,' she said, handing it to me. 'Don't spend a penny on anything else.'

She thought it would be cheaper to buy a bit of material and have a dress made up instead. But I couldn't be bothered and wanted something ready to wear. I was sick of black. I'd been wearing it since the funeral.

Just before I left for town the post arrived. I bounded downstairs as it came through the letter box.

'If it's more bills I don't want to know,' my mother called from the kitchen. Sure enough they were all bills except for one addressed to me with an English postmark. I pounced on it, knowing it was from Clair and hid it in my pocket as my mother came out to the hall.

'Remember now, everything has to be black,' she said

and, drying her hands on her apron, shuffled through the bills.

'Don't worry, I know,' I said smiling my head off.

'What's there to smile about with all these to be paid,' she wanted to know.

'I'm off,' I said unable to stop smiling. I was all lit up and mad to read the letter, but not till I got on the bus. The writing was slightly slanted, even and clear. He'd posted it two days ago when I was in black despair. Now I was singing inside and looked at it in wonder. He had written it, touched it, licked the envelope and sent it to me.

The letter was short, barely a page. There was a Postal Order for five pounds enclosed. My share of the prize for the short story competition. I was amazed. Imagine writing something and winning a prize for it. It was decent of him to share his winnings. I hated boys who were stingy.

He sounded happy. It was easy to get work, and he'd found a job and somewhere to live in the first week. It was only a room, but it had a piano and a balcony. He said the house was full of musicians so there was no problem about noise. Why didn't I come over for a bit? He signed his name with an 'X' underneath.

The bus dropped me at the top of Grafton Street. I bought some notepaper and envelopes and sat in Bewleys sipping coffee in a daze. I kept reading his letter over and over again till I had it by heart. There was loads I wanted to ask. What was it like over there? Were the people nice? What were the girls like? Were they amazing-looking? Did he meet any at work? Was he homesick at all? Instead I wrote this really boring letter about the weather, the hat-modelling job, and the shop being sold. Then I wandered around looking for something to wear but the shops were full of bright summer clothes. There was nothing in black, only middle-aged stuff like my mother wore. I'd probably have to get some material and a pattern after all.

In Arnotts I found myself in a department called Bottom Drawer where I watched a mother and daughter with their heads together going over a list. I followed them, amazed at how well they got on. They had the same taste and agreed with each other about everything. Apart from their age difference, they even looked the same.

I envied the silky lace underwear they were choosing. It reminded me my own was in bits. I picked out a bra that seemed about right. It was so long since I'd bought one, I wasn't sure of the size. In the changing room a notice said: OUR ASSISTANTS WILL BE PLEASED TO MEASURE YOU ON REQUEST.

No fear, I thought. They looked so old and glum and I was afraid they'd see the grey rag of a bra I'd taken off. The one I tried on was black trimmed with ribbons and lace. It fastened in the front and gave me such a cleavage I had to have it at once. Then I chose matching underpants, a suspender belt and black nylon stockings with seams. I paid for the lot with one of Father Brian's five-pound notes and wondered what they'd think, my mother and himself, about my new rig-out. But then they had insisted that everything had to be black.

Back in O'Connell Street I passed a shipping office and without thinking went in and asked the price of a ticket to London.

'Single or return?' the man asked.

'Single, it'd be cheaper,' I added with a blush.

'Four pounds ten,' he said giving my stomach a look.

Does he think I'm pregnant or what? I wondered and, handing over Clair's fiver, booked a ticket for Saturday night.

You fool, I told my thumping heart. What d'you think you're doing? They'll be after you like a shot. You're underage. They'll bring you back. Another voice said, I don't give a damn, I'm going. I'll change my name. Nobody'll stop me.

With this going on, I went into Clerys and managed to find a nightdress for nine and six. It billowed out like a tent, but it was all I could afford. It wasn't black. It wasn't any colour at all. It was completely transparent, but then Clair had said, it's what's inside that counts. Maybe I'd just wear it in the dark or under the bedclothes. It felt soft to touch.

When I got home I told my mother I'd bought some material and a pattern and left them up with the dressmaker.

Chapter 27

The drone of the Hoover sounded from the house. I sat in the garden on one of the fireside chairs trying to get a tan for London. I felt guilty because I was going away and my mother was killing herself spring cleaning.

She wouldn't let me help. She had her own way of doing things and wanted no interference. Starting from the top of the house she was working her way down systematically, as she called it, stripping each room to the bare boards. Yesterday it was the curtains and covers and today it was the turn of the furniture.

Everything moveable had been dragged into the garden to air. The furniture looked shabby and ancient in the bright sunlight.

'You'd never think your father was in furniture,' my mother grumbled as she placed the worst pieces under the lean-to shed. The shed, a canopy of corrugated iron, had been put there to hang any patched and darned underwear she was too ashamed to let Gertie see.

The weather was still amazing. Everything in the garden had suddenly burst into bloom. My mother said it was unnatural for the time of year. We'd have to pay for it somehow. It felt weird to think I'd be in London the day after tomorrow. I'd hidden the ticket in my shoe. It looked worn already, but I was terrified they'd find it and try to stop me.

I slid off the chair on to the grass and went limp. The sun seeped through me blotting out all the fears I felt about going away. It'll be all right, I assured myself. Nothing will go wrong. My mother thought I was going to an all-night party the following night, and Rowan promised he'd drop the farewell letter through our door the next morning if I gave him my collection of asylum balls. By the time she read the letter I'd easily be in London.

She'd have a fit when she heard. She took all the English newspapers and was always going on about the dreadful things that happened there. Especially the White Slave traffic. London was the worst. It was full of respectable-looking men in bowler hats with poisoned darts concealed in their umbrellas travelling on trains on the look-out for suitable victims. At the flick of a switch they could release the dart and drug you senseless. God knows what happened to you after that. I often asked my mother what exactly they wanted a White Slave for, but she never answered.

I wondered what it'd be like over there. Clair lived in a place called Chalk Farm. It reminded me of rolling fields with white fences and cows hanging over them with bells round their necks.

A shadow fell over me blocking out the sun.

'Marian, wake up quick.' My mother nudged me with her slipper. 'Father Brian's on the phone. He wants to arrange something about Howth.'

'Well you can tell him I'm not going.' I rolled away from her into the sun.

'What do you mean you're not going? You must. He's a priest. You can't refuse him.'

'I don't care who he is,' I said, wondering how could she be so blind. Didn't she know what he was after?

'You're being perverse, just like your sister, and after all he's done for us.' She rolled her eyes to heaven. 'God grant me patience, what'll I tell him?'

'Tell him I'm dying with my periods and I'd sink like a stone if I went for a swim.'

'Show some respect, Marian, I could never tell a priest anything like that. Anyway there was no mention of swimming,' she said her voice rising.

'Ssssshhhh,' I cautioned her. 'Gertie's in the garden.'

She stood there working her teeth up and down in annoyance. They came to rest with a clatter. I watched through the corner of my sunglasses her angry face soften as she thought up some excuse to tell Father Brian.

She wouldn't speak to me for the rest of the day. When I offered to get the tea she said not to bother with hers, it'd only choke her.

I lay in bed that night listening to her banging about downstairs. It was awful to be rowing on our last night. Things hadn't been so bad lately. Especially since Celine went off to work in Butlins. We'd a row before she left over her padded bra which she accused me of stealing. Of course I'd borrowed it, but couldn't let on or she'd have killed me. It was too late to put it back in her drawer. She went round like a demon looking for it.

'Sure what would she need a bra for? She's nothing to put in it,' my mother asked like a fool.

'Yes she has,' Celine snapped.

My shoulders shot up defensively as they eyed my chest.

'So she has, dear,' my mother said noticing them for the first time.

'Unless they're stuffed,' Celine said spitefully.

'You'd know more about it than I would,' I said reminding her of the time she stuffed her bra with lime-green stockings for a dress dance and they'd crept up around her neck during the night like snakes. Her partner, a bit pissed, said for a joke that he thought St Patrick had banished them all from Ireland.

Celine stamped her foot in a rage. She refused to go to Butlins without her bra. My mother put her arm around her and offered to help her find it. Celine shrugged her off angrily and they went up to her room to look. While they were there I dropped the precious bra behind the laundry basket in the bathroom.

Later I felt guilty as I wouldn't be seeing her for ages. I offered to hear her lines. She was auditioning for an American play and had this fake accent that got on my nerves. Maggie, the part she was reading, was crazy about this guy who drank like a fish. He wouldn't give her the time of day. In the end she said she'd stick a knife through her heart if she thought he'd never make love to her again. Celine kept getting it wrong and got really annoyed. She couldn't understand why Maggie wanted to stick the knife in her own heart instead of her man's. She went over it a million times until she got it right.

Before I left her, I asked how she felt about our father. Did she miss him a lot?

'I don't miss him at all.'

'Oh,' I said surprised.

'Well, he comes and visits me whenever I want.'

Jesus, I thought, what's she on about. Is she off her head? I decided to go along with it. Part of me wanted to believe he was still there somewhere, but the rest of me wanted to run a mile.

'He never visits me,' I said, playing her along.

'Why would he? You don't deserve it,' she snapped and I realised she wasn't joking at all. 'At first I wouldn't let him in, but then I thought, what the hell.'

'How was he?' I asked.

'Embarrassed.'

'Why?'

'I've never let him into my room before. He admired my new outfit for Butlins and was proud I was always in work.'

'Did he look well, was he happy?' I asked.

'I dunno. I didn't notice. We had a row.'

'Why?'

'He wanted to go to the pub.'

'You bloody liar,' I said and nearly hit her with the book. 'Stop acting for once and looking for notice. You're only making it up.'

She looked at me with fear, something I'd never seen before.

'Maybe I am, I dunno. Sometimes I forget when I'm acting and when I'm not.' This really put the wind up me and I was glad when she left.

Now I was rowing with my mother. I hated leaving her like this but she could keep it up for days and I couldn't wait that long. Clair might meet someone else, I thought and remembered the time he went off with that girl at the party. God knows what sort of exotic creatures he might meet in London.

Next morning I brought her up breakfast. She'd moved into my father's room. It was strange to see her in his bed. There wasn't a trace of him left. Even the smell was different.

'What's this in aid of?' she asked, eyeing the tray suspiciously as she heaved herself upright.

'Nothing, it's just you've been working so hard.' I steadied the tray as she reached for her teeth on the dressing table. She looked vulnerable without them.

'What kind of a day is it?' she asked in that polite I'm-not-really-talking-to-you voice.

'Another scorcher.' I drew the curtains back for her to see. The sun poured down into the garden. My beech tree was covered in pale green leaves. I won't see them change this year, I thought with a stab.

'Has Gertie got her washing out yet?' my mother asked, her voice harsh with the teeth.

'I think so,' I said, noting the full load on the line next door.

She banged down her cup. 'Here, hold this and hand me my glasses.'

I held the tray steady while she put them on.

'Have you ever seen Gertie without her glasses?' she asked.

I shook my head.

'She looks dreadful. They're the only thing that holds her face together.' She whooshed herself up on the pillows and strained to see out the window. 'I declare to God she always beats me to it. I don't know how she does it. She must have been up since the crack of dawn, or else got Basil to do it. How that man hasn't collapsed long ago is a mystery to me. Out all day at work and then having to come home to that?'

I edged out the door. 'Let me know if you want anything.'

She called after me, 'Leave out any dirty clothes you have for washing.'

I'd hardly any clothes so there wasn't much to pack,

just a few tops and skirts, and of course the new nightdress and underwear.

She was in the kitchen when I went to say goodbye. She looked weary standing over the sink washing the clothes. I hated saying goodbye like this, but it was the only way. She started when she saw me.

'God Almighty, Marian, what are you doing standing there? You put the heart across me.'

'Why are you so nervy when anyone's at the door?' I asked.

'I don't know what you mean.'

'It's true. Any time there's a knock at the door you jump.'

'Well, I wasn't aware of it,' she said and pummelled the clothes so hard the suds slopped on to the floor. 'Now would you leave me alone, I've got work to do. Gertie Freeney's had her washing out hours ago.' She wrung out a towel, twisting it till there wasn't a drop left.

I went to put my arms around her. 'Will you be all right tonight?'

She stiffened. 'Of course I will. Why wouldn't I be? I've never fallen out with my own company.' She pulled away from me, the way she always did when my father tried to hug her, and plunged both hands in the sink. She flicked the suds aside to reveal the dark water beneath. 'Would you look at the filth I've got out of these curtains. Have you ever seen anything like it?' She sounded pleased.

'I'm off now.' I waited hoping she'd turn so I'd get a last look at her face.

She turned to me questioningly. 'Where does it come from? That's what I'd like to know?'

'What?' I asked puzzled.

'Dirt.'

'I dunno,' I said and was about to leave when the phone rang.

My mother dried her hands and went to answer it. I hung around waiting.

She came hurrying down the hall in a fluster. 'It's for you, Marian.' She looked surprised. 'A Mr Lyall, something to do with films.'

'Never heard of him,' I said and went to answer it.

'This is Ronnie Lyall, personal assistant to Mr Seaman,' a smarmy voice said. 'Mr Seaman's in town casting for his new film, *Robin Hood*. He asked me to call you and request the pleasure of your company for dinner one night.'

He waited. I didn't know what to say. All I could think of was Monty Seaman's big belly and cowboy boots with spurs.

'He has you in mind as a stand-in for Maid Marian and perhaps even a small part as well,' the voice went on.

'Hold on a minute,' I said knowing exactly what Monty Seaman had in mind.

'What does he want?' my mother said excitedly.

When I told her she nearly jumped out of her skin. 'Go on, take it. Say yes. Don't keep them waiting.'

I can't, it's impossible. What'll I say? I thought quickly and took my hand off the mouthpiece. 'Does it mean I'd have to ride a horse?' I asked.

My mother's eyes widened with fear. I'd fallen off a horse once and lain unconscious for hours. She'd made me promise never to ride one again in my life.

'What'd he say?' she whispered anxiously.

'He's gone to find out.'

'Maybe if they tied you on,' she suggested.

'Are you mad?'

Mr Lyall came back and said yes, it would mean riding a horse.

'In that case,' I told him, 'I couldn't possibly but thanks all the same.' He left a number if I changed my mind. I pretended to take it and put the phone down.

'It's a terrible shame to let a chance like that go,' my mother said.

I could see she was torn to pieces between telling me to risk it, and fear in case I fell again and broke my neck.

'Can't be helped.' I kissed her on the cheek. 'I've to go now.'

She said goodbye absentmindedly, still in a quandary, wondering if she'd done the right thing.

There was no one at the bus stop. I must have just missed one. In a panic I walked up and down terrified I'd be late for the boat. Don't be ridiculous, I reasoned, there's two hours to go and it only takes an hour to get to Dun Laoghaire.

That's if it hurries up and comes. A car passed and slowed to a stop. I ran after it thankfully. It was funny, I'd been lucky with lifts lately. Boys I barely knew stopped. It'd never happened before.

When I got to the car and saw Father Brian sitting there I nearly died.

'Where are you off to?' he asked.

'Dun Laoghaire. I've a hair appointment,' I lied, 'and I'm late.' I stood there gaping like a fool clutching my hair.

'Hop in then, I'll take you.'

'But where are you going?' I stalled.

'Anywhere you want.' He waved his hand expansively.

I got in reluctantly. The car looked expensive and smelt of leather and cigars. It didn't seem like a priest's car. A bottle of suntan lotion sat on the dashboard.

'Congratulations on getting the job,' Father Brian said and reached across me to lock the door. He patted my knee and left his hand there.

I pulled away and said, 'It's not what you know, it's who you know.'

He laughed. 'Mr Hare's extremely influential, a good person to know.'

Like yourself, I thought.

'What happened yesterday? Your mother said you were suddenly taken ill.'

'Too much sun. I'm not used to it.'

'You look all right today,' he said taking in the blue silk sheath dress I'd borrowed from Celine. She left it behind and I was going to send it back. I had to look my best when I met Clair.

'What d'you say we celebrate and head for Howth. We could check out some hotels, and go for a swim. The weather's great.'

To my horror, before I could say anything he swung left into town, instead of right down Eglinton Road.

'I'm sorry, I can't,' I said getting all agitated.

'Relax, surely your hair can wait. The job doesn't start for another week. A dip will do you good.'

'But I haven't a bathing costume or anything,' I said weakly.

'You must have something in that bag of yours,' he said, eyeing my bag on the floor.

I crunched it under my feet remembering the underwear I'd bought with his money. 'Thanks for the loan by the way, I'll pay it back.'

'Don't mention it. Look on it as a gift, an investment in your future.'

We paused at some traffic lights. It was only then I realised we had to pass through town to get to Howth. A bus from the Pillar would take me straight to the boat.

Cars had pulled up alongside us. People saluted Father Brian. He bowed his head and gave them his blessing. Pious hypocrite, I thought, and cringed. The lights changed. We drove on.

'Do you really need a bathing costume, Marian? I know lots of little coves and places where we can be private.' He turned to me and smiled. It was more of a leer.

We were coming into College Green. 'That'd be nice,' I heard myself say. 'But not today. The thing is, it's embarrassing really, but I have my monthlies. I must get to a chemist quick.'

All the smugness left his face. He reluctantly pulled the car over to the kerb.

'This'll be fine,' I said fumbling with the door.

He reached across and released the catch. 'If you're sure then?'

'Yes, thanks.'

'You'll be all right for the weekend, though. I'll give you a ring to arrange things,' he said recovering himself.

'That'll be great,' I said.

'God bless,' he added.

I waved before slamming the door and disappeared into the nearest shop which turned out to be an Imco dry cleaners.

*   *   *

I was quaking when I got to the boat. A policeman and an inspector stood by the gangplank. Although I'd paid the full fare, I was sure they'd stop me for some reason. This is it, I thought as I handed up my ticket but they let me pass.

The lounge was full of chattering people. Everyone seemed to be travelling with someone. Children raced about shrieking up and down the aisles. A group of tinkers lay sprawled round the empty bar having a sing-song. Someone joked there'd be no excuse for puking it all up on the way over. The sea was like glass. A woman sat alone by the window surrounded by luggage. I sat near to her.

'They're starting early,' she said, nodding to the tinkers. 'I'd steer clear of them if I were you. They'll turn nasty later on. If it's anything like last time even the crew were afraid to interfere.'

'Do you go over often?' I asked.

'I live there now.' She smiled. 'I'm married to an Englishman. They make wonderful husbands. Much better than the likes you'd get over here.'

She patted her hair. It grew dead flat on the top of her head, as if a heavy weight had lain there for a long time.

'He's very good to me you know. Lets me over to visit my people whenever I want, and he's so good with the girls. Money's no object.'

A commanding voice over the loudspeaker read out a list of names asking them to report to the purser's office immediately. I couldn't make half of them out with all the noise.

'What are they wanted for?' I asked the woman uneasily.

'Oh, just last-minute messages from relations and

friends.' She drew the tips of her coat together over her knees to form a perfect square.

Christ, suppose Rowan's weakened and shown the letter to Gertie. She'll be round hot foot to my mother.

'When do we leave?' I asked the woman.

She consulted her watch. 'Twenty minutes to go.'

I must hide, I thought, and went to stand up. A woman with a determined look on her face weaved her way towards me carrying a notebook. 'I'm from the Catholic Youth Society. Have you an address to go to in London?' One of her eyes focused on mine, the other wavered disconnectedly across the room. I followed it with the vague hope she might be talking to someone else.

'Yes,' I said nodding for safety.

'A Catholic home?' she went on.

I nodded again.

'Good, good. What district will you be living in?'

'Chalk Farm.'

'Let me remind you of your nearest Catholic church,' she said, leafing rapidly through her notebook. 'Let's see. That'll be St Dominic's Priory. Father Cooney's parish.' She wrote the address down. The loudspeaker started again, more urgently this time.

'Excuse me please.' I stood up as she pressed the address into my hand.

'Be sure and contact Father Cooney first thing. God bless.'

The metal door of the Ladies' room clanged shut muffling the voice over the loudspeaker. I locked myself in a cubicle determined to stay there until the boat sailed. There was a faint smell of vomit. I flushed Father Cooney's address down the toilet. A grinding noise rose from somewhere deep within the bowels of the boat. The cubicle shuddered. Is it moving at last? I wondered and ran upstairs and out on deck. The boat was moving. People hung over the sides waving to friends below on the pier. I watched the land slip away as the boat swung round and manoeuvred its way through the mouth of the harbour.

The sun, a giant ball dipping into the sea, threw a rosy light over everything. I looked back and saw the city lying snugly beneath the Dublin mountains and remembered the walks I'd had there with my father. Where is he now? I thought. Nowhere, he's gone for ever. Everything became a blur as my eyes filled up. I turned away. Overhead the gulls wheeled silently following the boat. I wondered where they lived, did they have a home, or were they always flying backwards and forwards without settling anywhere? I saw the little island where Clair and I had spent our day together, and beyond, stretching for ever, the white line of the horizon.

This time I'll live, I thought. Even if it kills me.